Gospel, Grits, and Grace

*Encountering the Holy in the Ridiculous,
Sublime, and Unexpected*

T. Wyatt Watkins

Illustrated by Donna U. Watkins

Judson Press
Valley Forge

Gospel, Grits, and Grace: Encountering the Holy in the Ridiculous, Sublime, and Unexpected

© 1999 by Judson Press, Valley Forge, PA 19482-0851

All rights reserved.

Unless otherwise noted, Bible quotations in this volume are from the New Revised Standard Version of the Bible, copyright © 1989 by the Division of Christian Education of the National Council of the Churches of Christ in the United States of America. Used by permission. All rights reserved. Other Bible quotations are from *The Holy Bible*, King James Version.

Library of Congress Cataloging-in-Publication Data

Watkins, T. Wyatt.
    Gospel, grits, and grace : encountering the holy in the
ridiculous, sublime, and unexpected / T. Wyatt Watkins : illustrated
by Donna U. Watkins.
        p.   cm.
    ISBN 0-8170-1311-3 (pbk. : alk. paper)
    1. United States—Social life and customs—20th century—Fiction.
2. Rural churches—United States—Fiction.   3. Rural clergy—United
States—Fiction.   4. Christian fiction, American.   5. Humorous
stories, American.   I. Title.
PS3573.A8447G6   1999
813'.54—DC21   98-50165

Printed in the U.S.A.
06   05   04   03   02   00   01   99
10   9   8   7   6   5   4   3   2   1

To my mother and father,
Genie and Bedford Watkins,
from whom I first experienced
the true meaning of grace

Contents

One
STAGE SETTINGS
When cats and dogs are thrown together,
curious things begin to happen.

Two
SAINTLY SINNERS
It's not who you know, but how you meet up
with God through their acquaintance.

Three
SACRED SPACES
Every inch of earth is shot through with the holy,
and through the holes we steal a peek at heaven.

Four
SENSITIVE SITUATIONS
You can get there from here,
but you have to pedal backwards.

Five
SINGULAR SPIRITS
Faith regards tragedy
through the lens of redemption.

Six
SANCTIFIED SEASONS
We script our lives in liberty, but each successive
scene is free playing its way back to God.

Acknowledgments

A first-time author has more words of gratitude to share than could be contained within the pages of his whole first volume. The urge to write had flared up inside me like an irresistible itch that only a sharp #2 pencil (or the click of very crisp computer keys!) could satisfy. While the world of Ashgrove Baptist Church nudged its irksome way into my mind and heart, I struggled to discern how to honor it with a wider hearing. Without the constant guidance and support of so many souls, neither I nor the good folks of Ashgrove would be welcoming you at our door!

I am thankful to my agent, Georgia Hughes, both for her insightful assistance and because she believed in my work when I was most beset by doubt. My thanks also to Robert Maccini, who took the initiative to share my stories with Laura Barrett of Trinity Press, who, in turn, was kind enough to pass them along to Judson Press. I am very grateful for the many willing hours of encouragement and guidance I have received from my editor, Randy Frame, and the fine editorial staff at Judson Press, as work on this book progressed.

I am indebted to the people of the churches I have served, and especially to the Emerson Avenue Baptist Church, which graciously granted me the sabbatical on which this project was completed. My deep thanks, as well, to my dear friend, Dr. D. Newell Williams, who offered many helpful suggestions as the manuscript developed.

I am most especially grateful for the keen eyes of my mother, and those of my father, who, as a poet, is my inspiration, and who has been as well my most ardent supporter—and of course my four dear children, who endured my distraction with the voices who kept calling from *the little grove of maple and ash.*

Finally, I share my unbridled delight at the gift of creative collaboration with my wife, Donna, illustrator of these stories and lifetime love, whose gift of *sight* still leaves the preacher speechless.

The goodness of God and the faithful struggles of God's people remain the best stories told. Should the tales here contained shed any further light on the brilliance of the Gospel, already ashine, then I and all the saints of Ashgrove Church commend that good fortune to the greater glory of God.

Preface

How have we arrived where we are in life? It is a curious mixture of choice and chance, mysteriously stirred by divine intent. When we are young, the book of life is opened wide. We flip its pages blithely, unaware that each can be turned only once, and all lead to the same inexorable ending. Age brings a chastened view of time and opportunity. If we are watchful, we begin to glimpse in each average, even irksome, episode a touch of the sublime, to see each chapter tinged with the holy. We come to recognize the light of God shining through all things.

In the mid-1980s, I followed the muse—some of us call it the Spirit—to a little church out on the county's edge, situated in a grove of maple and ash. Fresh from seminary, I was eager to leave my mark on the great map of Christian endeavor. It was a surprise to no one so much as to me that my pastoral charge was on uncharted ground. I became caught in a clerical crucible, the ecclesial equivalent of boot camp. I was a city dweller stranded in the country, an activist marooned on an island of complacency, and a theological moderate caught one notch too tightly in the grip of the Bible Belt.

One-half of the church membership was related, and one-half was from Kentucky, and it was the same half. Among congregational distinctives, nothing rivals the impact of blood relation. When it flows from Kentucky, that blood carries a special potency. And the discreteness of the Kentucky drawl left me as baffled as my first day of beginner's Greek.

I arrived, steeped in theological theory, yet to be distilled to the level of country life. I raised the question of theodicy; folks were confronting serious evil, daily and personal. I waxed eloquent on the theme of God's forgiveness; they had aunts, uncles, and cousins, sisters and brothers, moms and dads with whom they had not been on speaking terms for decades. I spoke of world peace; they drove pickups toting chrome-plated gun racks. I preached tolerance; they could scarcely tolerate it, and, truth be told, I barely could myself. The fact that pastor and people connected at all remains the best evidence I have that the Light still shines, that life is still held in the clutches of grace, that God is alive and well and living in hearts.

This book is about one peculiar mingling of earth and heaven, in the persons, places, and events of a little church in a grove, a place that now resides deep down within me. The stories that follow, like most I have heard, are blendings of truth and fable, fact and fiction. Some of them occurred much as told. Others, to the best of my recollection, never happened at all. Most fall somewhere in between. As to which ones are which, I leave this to the reader's imagination. At times I can barely recall myself. And who is to say whether, given the time and the opportunity, those events that have not yet come to pass are slated to happen next? After all, today's musings may be tomorrow's miracles—at least, for eyes of faith.

Introduction

Human experience unfolds in story. Meaning is fashioned from places, plots, and players, fused in real time. *Gospel, Grits, and Grace* is a contemporary rendering of the message of the Christian gospel in story. It is based on encounters from my first pastorate, by which I clarified for myself some core meanings of the Christian faith. Chief among these is this: that the church at its best comes down to ordinary people in average places saying and doing things of great, sometimes divine, moment. This book is a pastor's reckoning with one such mingling of earth and heaven in the persons, places, and events we call "church."

Some stories herein are "insider baseball," realities expressly for the community of the gathered. Others address universal experiences, such as tolerance, forgiveness, illness and death, tragedy and hope. Still others wrestle with live issues from the societal main, as they challenge the ethos of the church in general and each congregation in particular. Included among these are such things as the impact of technology, class distinctions, urban-rural tensions, race, and human sexuality.

All of these stories are governed by a strong if implicit preference for grace over judgment, by the bid for unity amid diversity and by an abiding faith in a God who is present and active in all reality. They are not intended to preach or moralize. Instead, they aim to delight and uplift, to arouse thoughtful reflection, and, most of all, to tell the truth about how things are or might be.

Through the ordinary everydayness of place, plot, and people, *Gospel, Grits, and Grace* attempts to illumine something of the extraordinary and the transcendent, which are everywhere present for the vigilant to see and share.

ONE

Stage Settings

Let the favor of the Lord our God be upon us,
and prosper for us the work of our hands—
O prosper the work of our hands!

Psalm 90:17

When cats and dogs are thrown together,
curious things begin to happen.

1

Over Good Earth

We'll Clear Us Some Land and Raise Us a Steeple!

. . . the LORD God made the earth and the heavens, and every plant of the field before it was in the earth, and every herb of the field before it grew. . . .
Genesis 2:4–5 (KJV)

Life pushes out, or it is pushed out. When a full-term baby refuses to vacate the womb, Pitocin may be administered, coaxing the little life to swim out to a much bigger pond. In a holy huff, God shoved Adam and Eve over the garden wall, but one supposes that, given the time, they or their progeny would have found a way out on their own. Abram left Ur, Jacob fled Beersheba. Trees spread branches, cities sprawl. Wal-Marts pop up, shutting Kmarts down. Unless you were born a sea sponge, to move on is to live on, to stand still is to expire.

The little church was birthed in a beer garden on the near west side of the city of Indianapolis. The German Catholic proprietor swept it out in the wee hours and set a few dozen chairs in rows, fashioning the sacred from the profane by sunrise. Then he slept, having safely secured a fair Sabbath's dispensation even in the Baptist view. This arrangement endured until the early 1920s, when prohibition turned everything upside down, particularly the beer steins. The congregation hastily threw up a modest building a few blocks away, but soon the state's right of eminent domain to erect public buildings displaced the

3

congregation a second time. Intending never again to have their noses closed in their hymnals by happenstance, the family of believers leapfrogged the entire twelve miles of county to the west. They bought land, cleared it, and planted a church with neither pubs nor public buildings in sight.

Of course, no people resided within view of church property either. Other than the core faithful, willing to drive across town in exercise of their hard-won sovereignty, there was no membership pool on which to draw. The mission field was comprised of coon and possum, crow and pheasant, and the odd pack of wild dogs. Beyond that, all was woods and cornfield. Few prospects ever found their way inside for a serious look around, and the ones who did were field mice. When the old hymn "Bringing in the Sheaves" was sung, the sentiment was palpable and veritable.

Yet the earth was good. The ground was fertile and the trees were of old growth. A heat pump and well, necessitated by the absence of city utilities at that distance, performed their functions better than half the time. Never during worship did the distressing sounds of the city, from sirens to angry shouting in the street, dampen the spirits of the faithful.

But ambivalent reality loomed on the horizon. Life pushes out. The city was coming.

It might take a dozen years or a score or more. But the city would stretch out its icy arms like a glacier, unsettling all in its path. The little church, nestled in a quiet grove of maple and ash, would have to be alive when it happened, and awake and ready.

In Due Course of Time

It screamed over the county line like an alien presence, invading airspace a mere twenty car lengths ahead of me. Wing flaps lowered, and landing gear dropped down with a high-pitched screech chilling enough to chase a banshee back into her grave. Its steely fuselage threw back the rays of a blinding sun until my tears washed away all sight. The jet turbos roared ahead to the right as the giant bird listed toward the runway of the Indianapolis International Airport. In a blind stupor, I swerved across lanes on the County Line Road, nearly ramming a concrete column at the entrance of a long drive. With a hard right turn, I skidded to a halt on a bed of bleached gravel. Squinting, I could just glimpse the craft as it whisked over a great fence of chain link, skirting airport property as far as the eye could see. A stand of trees at the perimeter bent down deferentially under the blast. They bowed and curtsied in all directions, as though the incessant takeoffs and landings had robbed them of all resolve to grow up straight and tall. Then all was still.

Wiping my eyes and glancing right, I followed the rise of an oversized steeple. It straddled the roof of a small frame church like a strong man riding a circus pony. As it had throughout the whole disquieting episode, the steeple stood proud and unperturbed. At its pinnacle perched a metallic cross, image of enduring love, of God's unyielding battle for peace waged in tumult.

Down below, at the entrance to the building, stood a committee of five who had witnessed the whole disturbing scene. Their mouths were closed tightly, but their expressions summed up a collective thought, roughly translated "City driver!" With a smile pasted hastily over considerable chagrin, I headed from the car and across the lawn in their direction.

"Wyatt Watkins," I announced. "How do you do?"

Immediately, their dispositions warmed, and hands were extended. A tall gentleman, the leader of the group, replied, "Come right on in, Preacher. Been waitin' for yeh. Welcome to Ashgrove Baptist Church!"

Seated at a large table in the fellowship hall, we commenced to deal out the cards of our lives to see what might match up. This was a tedious process for which such occasions are designed: my roots in Illinois, theirs mostly in Kentucky; I, with one brother in Chicago, they, from enormous families with a roll call of siblings numbering higher than some could count; my taste for classical music and European travel, theirs for country and western music from Nashville to Branson; my fondest passion, the church in the heart of the city; their greatest fear, the church in the clutches of the city; my interest in the new housing developments dotting the landscape; their anxiety over the same. The periodic flyover of another jet raised voices and assassinated entire thoughts in mid-sentence. An hour and a deck of odd cards later, the committee and I remained an unmatched pair.

Finally, over generous slices of pie, fresh-baked in a deaconess's kitchen with apples from her own tree, we began to bite into the real pith of the matter. I was a young minister seeking a start in an established church. They were an older congregation, in search of a fresh beginning. A church had weathered the decades of precarious quietude. Now, God had granted a season of storm and had even swept a young city preacher out along its leading edge, just to see if they were paying attention. Perhaps it was destiny, every bit as academic as apple pie. Before I left, they had asked me to candidate before their congregation, and I had heard myself accept. We shook hands and commended our course into God's care. Parting words were spoken. Stage and story were thus established. A most unlikely cast of players was assembled. An uncommon drama was set to unfold.

As I turned onto the county road, one last airliner shot overhead, as if in a stubborn effort to cleave the covenant God was forging between us. Its power to startle persisted but was no longer overwhelming. And visible through the rearview mirror, silhouetted in the setting sun, was a great steeple. It stood erect and unyielding, a beacon on a sea of rapid change and of seemingly irreconcilable differences.

2

The Study

Pastor under Glass

And they went away in the boat to a deserted place by themselves.
Now many saw them going and . . . hurried there on foot. . . .
As he went ashore, he saw a great crowd; and he had compassion
for them, because they were sheep without a shepherd.
Mark 6:32–34

It was an early Monday morning in June. The fog was still
lifting over sleepy fields. I pulled my '76 Pontiac Grand Le Mans
onto the grass and cut a path up to the entrance of Ashgrove
Baptist Church. This was my first day as a pastor. I had not yet
even received a front door key and was just pronouncing this trip
dead-on-arrival when Russ, the church custodian, appeared like
a genie in the mist. At the moment I popped the trunk, he
seemed to materialize out of thin air to unlock the building. Russ
was as part time as an employee can be, but he spent a great
many hours on church property anyway, since he had come
across nothing else of any promise to do with his days. Russ was
married with one daughter, Jenny. His wife, Polly, clerked at a
grocery store. With additional income from Russ's odd jobs,
done mostly for church folks, they eked out a living, if only
barely.

To my further good fortune, Russ committed the cardinal
error of snooping over for a look-see at what I was hauling.

"Lot a books yeh got there, Preacher."

"That's just the first load," I explained, "and they're
heavy."

"Well," he inflected with reluctance, ". . . use a hand?"
"Sure. Thanks."

We began to heave boxes into the small vestibule. Straight ahead east were doors that swung saloon-style into the sanctuary. Forward and to the right there opened a corridor to Sunday school rooms, the fellowship hall and the church kitchen. Just to the left, along the north wall, resided a large janitorial supply closet—"the office," as Russ enjoyed calling it. Hemmed in between "the office" and the back wall of the sanctuary was a somewhat smaller room. On the casing above the door, in large block letters, stenciled in gold, was a solitary word: *Pastor*.

"Well now," Russ comforted himself, " 'least we don't gotta lug them boxes up no humongous flight a' stairs!"

While candidating I had been permitted two brief peeks through the study door. On each occasion a premonition of warning, something on the order of a *Do Not Enter!* sign, had flashed in my head. These apprehensions had been stuffed like dirty laundry in a duffel bag. Prosaic concerns about location and square footage of an office had no place in the weighty matter of a pastoral call. Now, from across the threshold, things were taking on a somewhat different appearance. It was disconcerting that my inner sanctum sat right along the path of the Sunday morning stampede. How would I gather my thoughts and maintain my composure for the appointed hour? I needed privacy, solitude, space to think.

In my undergraduate days at Indiana University, the odds of tracking down professors in their offices had been roughly that of landing a starting spot on the squad of Bobby Knight's Hoosiers. The faculty enlisted human shields called teaching assistants to safeguard their time to do research. These reluctant gatekeepers, obsessed by their own dissertations and diplomas, were also avid practitioners of this great professorial disappearing act.

At seminary, professors' offices had been located along a second-floor corridor, cynically dubbed "heaven." Other than to the faculty lounge, the stairwell led to nowhere but their doors. Pausing on the first tread, students measured their words as if they'd been granted an audience with the Queen of England or the Dalai Lama.

And, of course, there was Jesus himself, who consistently sought time alone with God, though it seemed in his case to have come in short supply. For all his seemingly infinite power to call and convict, to preach and teach, to help and heal, Jesus never forgot the great whence of his mission. He never strayed far from the Source.

Now I was claiming a franchise in this business. This was the pastor's *study*—the seat of erudition, where originated words to cheer and chasten the church. It was the wellspring of congregational vision and mission, the fount where bubbled the wisdom of the ages. And this was a *pastor's* study—a place of prayer and of needful repose from the care of the flock. The study was to the church's shepherd as the sanctuary was to the sheep. It was Protestantism's "holy of holies," the place of priestly encounter with God.

But here at Ashgrove, the origins of things turned out to be somewhat less illustrious. Until recently this pastor's study had been the church's nursery. It had been placed adjacent to the sanctuary for the convenience of young families.

"That's why them windows is there!" Russ had intoned.

Into two of the study's walls, those shared with vestibule and sanctuary, had been inserted large panels of glass. They occupied a major part of each wall, thus converting the room into a veritable fishbowl. Their intent had been to put parents at ease, allowing them to check on their children without being observed. But the strategy had fallen victim to a serious miscalculation. On any given Sunday, pairs of little eyes would line the bottom edge of glass, peering out for any sign of Mom. Grownups were being closely monitored. The spying scheme had been inverted. During worship itself, moms could hear their babies crying through the glass. On sheer instinct they would turn clean around in their pews to find the little screechers staring them down, as they scratched at the glass like guinea pigs. This would unleash the kind of hysteria usually reserved for the outbreak of revival.

"But now that's all done been solved!" proclaimed Russ with satisfaction. "The little ones is all the way down the hall again, and the pastor's right up here where everyone can find him. . . ."

"What does that make me," I growled to myself, "a caged lion?"

Indeed, the glass inserts remained, fulfilling their original function with a fresh intent: pastor gazing.

In the 70s, Pontiac made its trunks as *deep* and *wide* as the fountain in the children's song by that name. Including those

cartons on the floor and passenger seats, we unloaded from the
car twenty-two boxes of books. It only took three of these to fill
the shelves of the study's only bookcase.

"Yes siree," said Russ, "looks to me like yeh got all the books
anyone could ever want right here, Pastor!" Then, in an encore
performance, Russ vanished into thin air as uncannily as first he
had appeared.

I stacked the remaining boxes along the study wall and sat
down to reconnoiter. Including another large window on the
outside wall facing north, my cubicle of a study had glass on
three sides. I was a wall away from being a cooked pheasant, and
out here the bird was on the menu. The remaining wall shared
a door with the custodial closet. Even as I noted this, a head,
Russ's, popped through it.

"Howdy there again, Pastor! Well, headin' out to mow grass.
Be seein' a lot a each other I 'spect! Bye!"

It was then that I caught an aromatic whiff of gasoline. In my
next equivocal breath, a full-blown plan began to rise like sweet-
smelling perfume. In addition to the lone bookcase, a small
desk, chair and lamp and a two-drawer filing cabinet were the
only office furnishings. The study needed a few things, and
among them were one by eights and cinder blocks. Bypassing my
home and hundreds of books that lay in waiting, I set a course
for Central Hardware. Then, with a center of gravity so low that
the rear tires flapjacked and the tailpipe scraped the road, I
drove back to Ashgrove Church. I built the bookshelf nearly to
the study ceiling, right up the center of the wall on the vestibule
side. In all, three hundred and thirty-nine books were successfully resettled, under the common classifications of a seminary library: theology, Christology, ecclesiology, biblical studies,
and practical ministry. The desk went under the south window,
buying me a lovely view of a sugar maple. The door to "the
office" I left closed but unlocked, confident that Russ, the
janitor-magician, could penetrate even concrete block if he so
chose.

The following afternoon I was greeted in the vestibule by
the chairman of the board of trustees. He was imposing, pot-
bellied, and pushing sixty. His name was Seymour, but he preferred Sergeant, or just Sarge, and folks were all too happy to
oblige him and more than a little afraid not to. Like many in the
church, Sarge's roots were all Appalachia, but he was an ex-
marine—though he would have denied there was such a thing.

Thus, his deportment was a peculiar mix of active passivity and passive activity. He had come to issue my church keys. They hung on a key chain connected to wooden praying hands. He was wearing the kind of smile intended to be mistaken for simmering anger.

"Mornin', Preacher. Say, what do yeh call that?" He was pointing to the study window.

"Looks like books," I replied.

"They're blockin' the window . . . and they're all turned around!"

"Well, it's my study, not a bookstore."

"Looks kindy bad, don't yeh think? You weren't thinkin' about leavin' 'em there. . . ." Other questions that weren't questions followed. I told him I would gladly talk over the situation with the board.

"Oh, no need," Sarge's tone softened. "The wife's been meanin' to sew up some curtains for them windows for two years now. Yeah, Millie's already done bought the material and everything—does fine work. Well, hope yeh like the key chain, Pastor. Whittled it myself!"

Weeks passed, but Millie wasn't making much progress on the curtains. Meanwhile, my heart, prone to be fickle, was revisiting the blurred boundaries of pastoral office. It was undeniable that the bookshelves did the vestibule no favors. I began to experiment with arrangements of books, interspersed by various knickknacks, especially the assortment of religious plaques members are always bringing to their pastors because they assume we appreciate that sort of thing more than normal people. These were faced strategically out the window, serving at least two purposes at once. Everyone seemed pleased, and my gimcrack benefactors were especially delighted.

Not long afterward, on a Sabbath morning prior to worship, the lion was in his den, preparing to meet visitors. I turned around at my desk to see a pair of eyes watching me intently through the glass between books and bric-a-brac. They were attached to Russ's daughter, Jenny, a specimen of freckles, curls, and cuteness all over. I walked to the bookcase with a grin and knelt down to eye level. Smiling back, she held up proudly the craft she had just completed in Sunday school. It was a pendant with praying hands. I fished out the key chain from my pocket, and we pressed our four hands up to the glass for a prayerlike moment. Then, in a flash, she disappeared from sight.

"Maybe it's in the genes," I posited. Quite unlike her father, however, Jenny was a lion tamer. Perhaps, if Millie's curtains ever got finished, I would think about leaving them open now and then . . . but not all the time.

> After saying farewell to them, [Jesus] went up on the moun-
> tain to pray.
>
> Mark 6:46

3

Prayer Breakfast

True Grits

*. . . and in the morning you shall have your fill of bread;
then you shall know that I am the LORD your God.*
Exodus 16:12

The men of Ashgrove Church gathered each Saturday morning for prayer and breakfast, not necessarily in that order of priority. This was already a five-year habit when I came onto the scene. At the outset, their wives had agreed to take turns in the church kitchen, scrambling eggs and frying bacon, pouring grease gravy over fresh-baked biscuits, or stacking pancakes five thick on bone china. The women had been quite taken with the whole business. To see their husbands engaged in anything at all of an overtly spiritual quality had itself been an answer to prayer. Still, they had supposed that this unprecedented display of devotion would "fetch up" after a few months. But a dozen or so of the most stubborn Joes in the congregation had fallen instead into a routine that augured the potential for longevity. It had begun to appear to the women that their culinary services might be required in perpetuity.

Meanwhile, these same wives had been of the growing opinion that Saturday morning had very little to do with prayer after all. Informal table conversations had left much to be desired. These had covered the calendar year of, for men, the most urgent concerns in life: planting weather and Indy Car racing in the spring; fishing, harvesting, and America's favorite pastime in the summer; football in the fall; and, all winter long, the great

Kentucky–Indiana basketball rivalry, which could generate enough heat to fry bacon and melt snow both at once. The prayer portion of the morning, the wives noted, could be so silent it made the Quakers sound loquacious, and it might be over before you could say "Pennsylvania Dutch." Any of these factors alone would have been good grounds for mutiny in the kitchen. When taken together, the breakfast in "Prayer Breakfast" didn't have a prayer.

The men had sensed their jeopardy. They moved to shore up support. Prayer requests from the congregation were invited and encouraged. Hasty attempts were made to engage the lofty questions of the faith. Bible study series were initiated. Study guides were purchased. Even a "Bring a Bible to Breakfast" campaign was engaged. Nonetheless, one by one, the newly devout of Ashgrove Church had regretfully informed the group of their wives' withdrawal from the Saturday morning cooking roster. The men were being quickly abandoned to cereal and toast. Without a real meal, it had seemed the whole affair would fold up like a poorly flipped flapjack. Then, to everyone's surprise, not the least their own, the men had determined to carry on alone—and to teach their wives a thing or two about *real* men's breakfasts in the process.

Things had begun well. Ed Garrett cooked pancakes and sausage and made them all proud, Kip Quarfarth proved to be an able omeleteer, though the crowd had to eat in shifts, and Rex Buchanan made tolerable French toast. But morale had been disappointment-racked, as well. Harold Hatch cooked a hot and spicy Mexican scramble with real jalapenos that everyone claimed to enjoy, but by the end of the day all had changed their minds. Junior Burges had the gall to serve instant oatmeal and was never asked to cook again, and Sarge Grimshaw's egg souffle almost burned the church down. After that, the men stuck to the stove top. It was at about this time that Jessie Calhoun had first ventured out to the little grove on a sleepy Saturday and managed to restore to the men's meeting a semblance of self-respect. His means were simple: *steak and southern grits.*

My first trip out to the Saturday men's prayer breakfast was a downright disaster. Donna, my wife, and I lived in the heart of the city, a full half-hour from the church. The prospect of spending both weekend mornings not only in the car but in the company of the Ashgrove flock was distressing to say the least.

And a scheduled event at 7:00 on a Saturday morning scaled the heights of absurdity. Three times that first morning our obnoxious alarm had propelled its pitiless whine into the delirium of dawn like a brick lofted through smoked glass. Three times I had crunched the snooze bar with the deadly accuracy of a seasoned slumberer. All the while, I had been occupied with a daybreaking dream—the kind you carry with you through the day like a scratchy throat. The dream seemed to have a future setting. In it I was *hanging* in the "Peanut Gallery" of former pastors. The men of the church were halted in front of me. They were accompanied by members of Jessie Calhoun's Elk Lodge, located two miles west into Hendricks County. Next, in that whimsical way of dreams, the Peanut Gallery seemed suddenly to metamorphose into a hunter's trophy room. Our men were busy showing off their latest kill, a prize of some note, a young buck. Its antlers were not yet fully pointed, but it was still a spoil worth some bragging rights. They were explaining that it had taken some effort, but in the end they had felled it and brought it back to hang up with the others. Then, just as my alarm clock sounded for a fourth and final time, it became creepily clear that the gallery and trophy room were one and the same. The young buck on display was me!

Aided by the forward ballast of antlers, I struggled free from my trophied captivity and bounded away to freedom. In real time and space, I had raised my heavy head off the pillow and, arms flailing, knocked the clock clean to the floor. The alarm had the last laugh: it was 6:25 A.M., and I was scheduled to "pray in" my first official men's breakfast at the stroke of 7:00.

Showerless, I sped away to the church, fighting back morning drowsiness and bargaining with God for a cup of coffee. When I reached the County Line Road, the rising sun beamed so brightly that I altogether missed the shape of a creature crouched in my path. Before I knew it, I had run over it with two tires. The possum writhed in the road pitifully before a pickup came along and finished it off.

I arrived at the church in spirits flattened like roadkill.

"You look white as a sheet!" Harold Hatch had said. "Somethin' hit you?"

"Sort of," I answered.

"You ready for breakfast?"

"Sure. What's cooking?" I asked. "Pancakes?"

"Well," Harold responded, "not hardly . . ."

Pancakes had sounded really good and, somehow, I had simply assumed they would be on a men's breakfast menu. Just at that moment, Jessie Calhoun had bolted from the kitchen bearing two large bowls brimming with a light yellow substance that looked forbiddingly familiar.

"Are those . . . *grits?*" I had gasped.

"Heck, no-ho-ho!" Jessie had chuckled to my momentary relief. "These here is *yaller* grits!—the kind Mama made down home."

"Jessie here makes the best *yaller* grits in Hendricks County!" commented Sarge Grimshaw, " 'cept my Millie's, a' course. . . . Cooks fer the Elks 'bout ever' other breakfast, and *you are go-nna love 'em!*"

Sarge uttered everything, including questions, in the declamatory. Yet, even for Sarge, there was an added dash of certitude in his voice.

For already two reasons—deer and possum—my morning appetite was prematurely curbed. Now had come a third: *grits.* My mother and father were both southerners. Not only did they appreciate a good bowl of grits, but they had gone to pains to instill in me a positive predisposition toward all gestures of hospitality. If it were offered at table, whatever it was, however well or ill prepared, you were to do your level best to eat it with a smile and to pay it highest compliment.

"Isn't that lying, Mom?" her eight-year-old son had once asked hopefully.

There were worse things than that kind of lying, she had answered, and one of them was rudeness with no good cause! Besides, she said, one never knew what might be at stake in another's kind gesture of hospitality.

As things turned out, I had recalled her words at quite the opportune moment. Only later did I learn of the prominent place of grits in the distressing story of Jessie Calhoun.

Jessie hailed from Franklin County, Tennessee. He had settled in Indiana after a falling out with an older brother, who stood to inherit their small third-generation family farm. The Calhouns were corn farmers. Jessie, though, had preferred hunting and livestock ranching. He had ventured out on his own against his father's wishes, hiring on at several beef cattle farms in counties west of home. His father had never spoken to him again.

When his father died unexpectedly, Jessie had uprooted and dutifully returned to the home place, intending to take up the slack. Instead, he had discovered that he was no longer welcome there. The scenario had smacked of the stories of Cain and Abel, Jacob and Esau, and the Prodigal Son rolled into one.

Meanwhile, a childhood friend had persuaded Jessie to try Indiana, so he had migrated to the western edge of Indianapolis. Here he had completed a tool-and-die apprenticeship and married an Ashgrove girl. In 1972, Jessie had joined the congregation, where he had served as a church trustee off and on for a decade.

Jessie and Ruthie Calhoun were now a devoted couple with three growing boys, but not once in fifteen years had Jessie mustered the nerve to return to Tennessee and the family homestead. Indeed, his only fond memories of the little corn acreage were of his mother and her cooking, especially hominy grits, ground from their own corn and soaked in the same lye from which she had made the soap he washed with before meals— sometimes. Perhaps it was in tribute to her memory that Jessie had taken up cooking the signature dishes of the South. Or maybe the sight, smell, and taste of them was the only way he had found to go home again. Either way, Jessie had become a self-styled, southern country gourmet in the North, distant enough from the nearest rutabaga patch to have distinguished himself, at least among the yokels.

Jessie's specialty was grits. He made them a dozen ways. There were grits with red-eye gravy, grits with cheddar cheese, and grits with onions and garlic. Jessie cooked them in bacon drippings, chock full of diced country ham, or straight, with steak on the side. He might prepare white grits with lots of butter and salt or sweeten them with sugar or syrup like the northerners do, or leave them plain as the plate they were plopped on. But Jessie favored the "yaller" kind, made from yellow corn— the corn his father had raised and his mother had shucked, hulled, and cajoled each morning into the best yellow miracle after the rising sun.

Grits to Jessie were more than something to chew up and swallow down like animal fuel. Grits were religion, a spiritual alchemy through which lost youth might be reclaimed at the onset of each new day. Grits were life.

Knowing none of this at the time, I owed a debt of gratitude to my *own* mother, who, while never subjecting me to grits in my childhood in Illinois, nevertheless instilled in me the *grit* to try almost anything.

At the breakfast table, I prayed that God might grant thankful hearts for a table spread. The watering of mouths and quick work of spoons established that any special need for such sentiment lay strictly with me. Then I gulped down a double helping of the yaller stuff with extra butter and salt. Bias aside, I had to admit Jessie's grits were better than good, and I told him so. While pleased by my appraisal, Jessie regarded it as a mere attestation to the obvious.

"Gooood, ern't they, Preacher!" Jessie said. "But next time yeh be sure ta' try 'em with lots a' syyyrup!"

Over the next few weeks, I puzzled out the pieces of Jessie's past, and an uncommon commonality between us came clear to me. While I was in no way estranged from them, my parents had retired from the North to their origins in the deep South, leaving their two grown sons singing "Yankee Doodle" in duet. Nearly every other relation on both sides of our family had an address below the Mason-Dixon Line. In a way, I was like Jessie, and together we shared with countless others the decimated sense of place, by then such a staple of modern Americana. We were children of the urban frontier, city sojourners seeking roots. And we had each found our way, by whatever lights, to the same little church near the border to nowhere. Now this tool-and-die maker from Franklin County, Tennessee, had introduced me to *true grits*, modern manna, this food of belonging that not only stuck to your stomach but bonded men into soul mates.

Four or so Saturdays later, it was again Jessie's turn in the kitchen. The turnout was especially favorable. I arrived clean shaven and well caffeinated. On the menu were steak and white grits. On the table were three jars each of A-1 Sauce and Aunt Jemima syrup, and two sticks of real butter. The men gathered expectantly around it with Styrofoam cups of piping hot coffee, chewing the fat while holding back the saliva of expectation. Fresh-squeezed orange juice sat at every place. When Jessie cooked, the cost share went up a couple greenbacks, but none minded. Once the bowls of steaming hot grits and slabs of slightly sizzled sirloin tip made their appearance, no time was wasted in blessing the feast before the gabby group fell into a long and necessitated silence. No food was wasted either. Each man ate according to his need—neither more nor less.

Yahweh had once enlisted Moses to feed the faint of heart in the desert. Now, with the help of Jessie Calhoun, holy manna had fallen once more into the lap of human necessity.

Grace and grits were conspiring to bring me safe thus far through an often inhospitable, modern wilderness. At a table of dwindling strangers, it occurred to me that, just maybe, they were likewise leading me home.

TWO

Saintly Sinners

*Do not remember the sins of my youth or my transgressions;
according to your steadfast love remember me,
for your goodness' sake, O LORD!*

Psalm 25:7

It's not who you know,
but how you meet up with God
through their acquaintance.

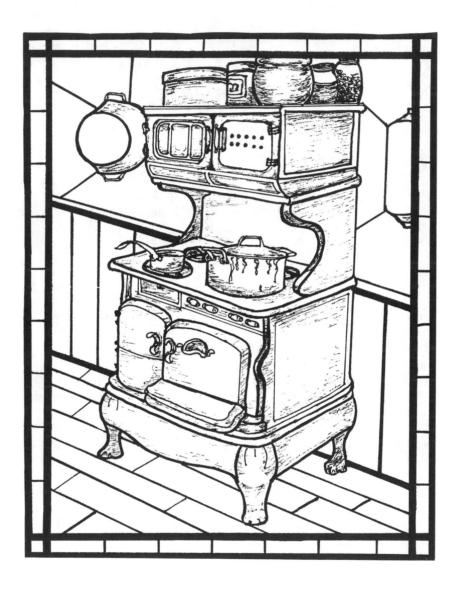

4

Bert

Southern Hospitality in Hell's Kitchen

. . . they broke bread at home and ate their food with glad
and generous hearts. . . . And day by day the Lord added
to their number those who were being saved.
Acts 2:46–47

Alberta Rump was on the squat side of weights and measures, but to look at her was to know she could have thrashed
anyone in the church at any time—man, woman, or beast. Her
face carried all the sternness of Appalachian women whom to
see is to be profoundly thankful they were not your mother. Her
eyes regarded you with grave suspicion. They were the kind of
eyes that would peer at you in the pulpit even when they were
shut, which was most of the time.

After my fifth Sunday, Alberta had proffered that my message was finally almost barely tolerable. People told me that with
this I should be very pleased.

When first I met Alberta, she called me "Preacher," and
Preacher was all I ever got. The name she instructed me to call
her, to her face at least, was "Bert."

Bert hailed from "somewheres" in Kentucky, and that
somewheres came north with her and now resided deep in her
soul. She lived in a poor district on the south side of the city
called Mars Hill. It was almost as if someone had known a
goddess of war would be coming. Her small, dirty white house
could be sighted from the interstate, where twenty years earlier
the expressway had barreled through, slicing up the residential

squalor of people with none of the pull up at city hall—Alberta's kind of people. Her yard was full of junk, probably lying in the exact spot it had been dumped off some ramshackle truck many years before. As far as anyone knew, no one had ever set foot inside the house except for Bert. Once a preacher had made it halfway through the front door, only to be forcibly repelled and sent packing, Bible shielding his backside.

Every Tuesday Bert was at church for the quilting bee. Six or seven ladies gathered around a large quilting frame in fellowship hall to preserve a way of life. Armed with stitching needles and thimbles, they passed their version of the Endangered Species Act from 9:00 A.M. till the stroke of noon. Then they set a table and held a solemn feast, a kind of victory meal, with nostalgia as the guest of honor.

I, too, was invited. In fact, my attendance there figured prominently in the unofficial job description of the pastorate. So each Tuesday I blessed the repast and ate for my trouble the best meal of the week by a beggar's mile.

The choice dish was Bert's chicken and dumplings. She fetched them to the church kitchen in a large pot, with thick broth dripping down the sides from sloshing around on the floor of her '72 Chevy Impala. Beneath a lardy film, simmering at the surface, were chunks of chicken the size of cube steaks and dumplings from scratch, plump as Bert's stubby fingers and five times as long. The pot sat over a burner on low, and the aroma snaked around the church, signaling the senses to full alert. It was better than any course from heaven's kitchen, and she knew it. Occasionally I caught myself worrying a bit about conditions in *Bert's* kitchen, but, hells bells, anything that tasted that good could tolerate a rogue bacteria or two.

Bert knew she had found the preacher's weakness and played it to full advantage. After services, before a dumpling day, she would greet me in the line with a simple, "Me 'n' the chicken 'n dumplin's be see'n ya Tuesday, Preacher." I also grew more confident toward Bert, believing that we had begun to develop a mutual understanding—likely something on the order of Nixon and Mao, but a diplomatic breakthrough nonetheless.

The moment of blessed assurance arrived one morning as I sat in my study. Bert surprised me at the door. I was bent over my desk in an attitude of prayer, and my words were just audible. Bert drew back in surprise and awe. I could just as well have been squishing a bug and gibbering to myself, but to Bert I was now a holy man, not a phony "like some them other preachers." As unlikely as it might have seemed to her, I was on a first-name basis with Jesus.

It was then that I determined to try it. She had surprised me; I would surprise her. I knew the house well from the interstate. I had found the exact spot on the wall map hanging in my study and stuck a pushpin clean through it. But access gained through that kind of dry run was not so easily repeated. After my first casual inquiry, Bert had issued stern warning never to come calling at her door. But I now fancied things to be different.

It was a chilly Monday before a dumpling day. The April sky was the kind of overcast that harbors no threat except to spit on you at any moment until you're damp to the skin but not soaked to the bone. So I parked several lots away from Bert's and approached the house on foot. From the look of things, an Alberta might have met me at each door on the block, or a Faye, or an Eva Lou, or an Ellie Mae. Old, overstuffed couches and home appliances lined every porch. Dotting front lawns were sorry-looking cars raised up on cinderblocks, like avant-garde sculptures too large for their pedestals, while dogs barked behind makeshift fences barely holding harm at bay. There was not a soul in sight, but I could feel the Appalachians themselves staring down at me.

Bert's car was parked only ten degrees off from square in a gravel driveway that ended abruptly at a poured concrete carport, harboring the odds and ends of indeterminate living. I traversed the yard to a small porch with a simple railing of curled iron. A rusty cowbell hung from a nail below the remnants of a hand-painted sign that might once have read *Wilkommen*. There was no evidence of a doorbell. I raised my right hand to knock. The rap of my knuckles on the storm door swore an oath to my ignorance for ever thinking to be there in the first place, while a fresh chorus of howling hounds was the jury pronouncing me guilty—or innocent by reason of insanity.

There was a long pause. I held fast to the iron porch rail just to keep from stealing away to the car and driving all the way to Key West without ever once looking back. Abruptly, two eyes popped into the single square of pane glass on the front door and stuck fast. Those eyes I had come to know so well just stared out at me. They divulged nothing about facial conditions immediately south, relegating my fate to my own terrible imagination. In a flash, I thought of the shotgun it was said she kept loaded

and of where, if toted at her waist, that would come up on me.
Never had I so regretted not carrying a Bible at my side on such
visits. Then, just as suddenly, the eyes were gone.

I stood like a deer in the middle of the road, frozen by the
headlights of impending doom. Finally, the door opened. "Hi,
Bert! . . ."

"Damn you, Preacher!" she interrupted, "Why'd you go
and do this?" What followed was an awkward silence. Lips
pursed in the strain of the moment, I was breathing through my
nose. In came the aroma of recollection. Chicken and dumplings! The scent of vindication. Bert was good at heart. Any soul
who cooked on a Monday for a Tuesday quilting bee was deep-
down sound. This was why I had come and why, even then, I felt
well-founded fear but not a tinge of regret. I turned to go.

"I'm sorry, Bert," I offered. "I really didn't mean to upset
you."

I was halfway across the lawn before she called down, "Day
early for dumplin's, Preacher. . . . Want some?"

It was only a few steps into chaos, but several long strides
into the reordering of hearts. At a kitchen counter surrounded
by clutter about which I am still sworn to secrecy, a preacher
prayed and two unlikely souls broke bread together in the smiling
sight of God.

5

Harriet

Blessed Nerve

Even though our outer nature is wasting away,
our inner nature is being renewed day to day.
2 Corinthians 4:16

Her flesh was numb as she typed—mostly a two-finger, hunt-and-peck affair. The neuropathy was always spreading to new regions of sensation. It heightened sensibility to the point of pain unbearable, then killed it down to a torpor, like a candle in the wind, burning furiously out of existence. Cigarettes dangled from her cracked lips, serial killers devoted in lengthy succession to their single victim. Her bifocal glasses were pushed down slightly on the bridge of her nose in that way that never fails to coax up the memory of some scolding school librarian. She fit the stereotype of the newspaper columnist, working as the world sleeps, papers stacked in heaps, trash can overflowing with innumerable wadded rejects, laboring from deadline to deadline. . . .

Harriet Crabtree was the editor of our weekly church newsletter, the *Link*. No visions or violent claps of thunder coerced here to take it on. Harriet had had the time and the machine. She had volunteered. Since then the little letter had grown into her reason to live another week. Now her life ticked away to the rhythm of an old Royal typewriter. Like Harriet, it was a real antique. Only its stubborn, mechanical action kept it from certain burial in open ground. The same might have been said of Harriet.

On Tuesdays, Harriet would hand over to me the newsletter draft, replete with coffee stains, tobacco ash, and smudges of food bearing clearer fingerprint samples than an FBI file. I had not easily mustered the courage to offer my services as copy editor. We tend to choose an uncomfortable course only when the alternative is more excruciating still. After a few weeks on the masthead of Harriet's work, I had come to believe that the alternative was to throw myself off the "crow's nest" of the church. Ever so gingerly, I had inserted myself between the first draft and the finished product and smiled my way through the ensuing season of adjustment.

I was a selective editor. Typos and misspellings were the symptoms to treat. The way Harriet and her machine could make the lines of type scroll up and down like a roller-coaster was fascinating but beside the point. This was battlefield triage. I could amputate letters and words, but not whole pages. A full third of the letter didn't change much anyway. For some time now, Harriet had honored every request for inclusion in the prayer list. There were church members and their relatives, neighbors, coworkers, and complete strangers, dogs, cats, and cockatoos. All were admitted. Most of the names were unknown to nearly everyone in the church. Some, whose illness was old age, had been listed there for five or six years. The record for longest duration on the roster was someone's great-aunt Loraine who, we later learned, was deceased for three years before having set it. We let the record stand. . . .

Each Wednesday morning I rang Harriet's doorbell, the letter with my corrections in a small, leather briefcase at my side. I was greeted by her old Chihuahua, Peekaboo, who was emboldened to bark her head off until I gained admission. Then she would retreat behind the davenport and make water. Harriet either never noticed or cared. Puddles of dried urine dotted the beige, sculptured carpet in a pattern of neglect.

Meanwhile, Harriet was eyeing the briefcase with suspicion, as if she expected scorpions to crawl out at any moment and sting her. We seated ourselves on opposite sides of her dining room table. Peekaboo sat on her lap, poised to come to her aid at the slightest provocation. With a click of my briefcase, the newsletter appeared. Slowly, I would push it across the table and into her hands, like a high-rolling financier making his last, best offer. Harriet's eyes stuck to the paper along its path and then studied it without visible expression.

Typically there would follow one of Harriet's trademark coughing spells. They could stretch out for up to ten minutes, during which time I dialed 911 repeatedly in my mind. The sound was excruciating, a high-priced filler of the awkward silence between us. When she regained her composure, I would wish her well and quickly excuse myself, backing out the door to avoid a final charge at my heels from her cranky canine.

Over time, it became apparent that each of Harriet's successive drafts only substituted new errors for the old ones. As in a shell game, one could never guess where these aggravating objects of anxiety might turn up next. But each Friday morning, ready or not, *The Link* was delivered in bulk-rate bags to the post office's central dispatch.

I was being delivered over to despair when someone donated the church's first computer—an Apple, with 48 kilobytes of memory. Immediately, a storage area was cleared and equipped with a computer table and work area.

Meanwhile, I was scheming a way to coax our little newsletter into the information age. I purchased a simple word processor and began to retype Harriet's first draft onto disk. The program was primitive by today's standards. As on many early computers, each line of text wrapped around the small screen, making the actual layout of each page a matter of guesswork. But it was light years beyond an old manual with butterfingers at the keys. These redrafts I began to deal out on Wednesdays at Harriet's dining room table. Pristine and smudgeless, they carried no red ink, no edits at all. Harriet's reaction was characteristically flat. Though we never discussed it, she took these to be final drafts, which she reproduced and mailed to the congregation.

Yet the absurdity of this weekly liaison between typewriter and computer was in the air. Sooner or later, Harriet would have to court the computer age or be led out to editorial pasture. So I prepared a friendly tutorial and invited Harriet to the church for Computer 101. It was a course in five parts, covering basic word processing, keyboard commands, retrieving, saving and printing.

Each session commenced with and ended in fervent prayer. Even so, Harriet flunked, and so did the computer. The click of the keypad lacked authority, she said, while the luminous screen gave her vertigo and the dot-matrix printer brought to mind the sound of a submachine gun. She began to cancel our Wednesday appointments. Her neuropathy was flaring up something fierce, she explained. And Peekaboo was ill and not eating.

I continued to develop the little letter on my own. Small feature stories were solicited from the membership. Short columns highlighted various congregational ministries. Someone supplied multiple reams of colored paper, and I began to leave space for clip art at the top of each article. *The Link* was becoming a refined little piece of journalism. But something was not right. Harriet and Peekaboo were by now spending their days in bed. Overflowing ash trays and half-empty coffee cups cluttered every flat surface within reach. Unchewed doggy treats littered the floor. Hour by hour, journalist and sidekick were failing. One of her nieces enlisted me to help persuade Harriet to go to the hospital. I pulled up a chair to her bed and held her hand, but no words of clarity came. The lump in my throat precluded speech on any account, and I felt the unease of guilt that itself refuses to answer to reason or consolation.

On a chilly Monday in March, Peekaboo died. She was wrapped lovingly in her favorite blanket and buried alongside the other canine souls in the pet cemetery on church grounds. Late that afternoon, the earth was covered with darkness. Thunder rocked the countryside around the little church. Lightning flickered across the faces of guilty and innocent alike. I was in the computer room, composing my weekly pastoral letter to the congregation, when it struck the roof and stirred my words like scrambled eggs. When power returned to the news room, all disk files, every word of composed text, all traces of the information age, had been mysteriously raptured out of existence. A single blast from heaven had quashed at least one line in the dubious advance of technology.

It had taken more than a little lightning and thunder, but now the path ahead was clear. Harriet had the time and the typewriter. She had volunteered. On the one backup floppy were the skeletal remains of Harriet's original newsletter. These I managed to pull up and print out, including the long-winded prayer list with the name of one Chihuahua deleted. Then I unplugged the computer from the wall.

That Wednesday, Harriet labored to the door and I entered the hush of a house in mourning. At her dining room table, I clicked open my briefcase and produced the single-sheet newsletter shell.

"Computer crash," I explained. "It's over."

Harriet said nothing. She didn't cough. She dusted off the Royal on the same day she got the carpet cleaned. Then, like a young journalist assigned her first feature story, Harriet got down to work. For better or worse, the fortunes of a struggling church and an antique typewriter were once again tightly bound.

Life was moving swiftly on ahead of us, caught in the juggernaut of technological progress. Clean, crisp, antiseptic words continued to flow out into the world in pentium torrents. This endless babble of 1's and 0's bombarded a billion souls in the twinkling of an eye, while our type trickled out like water from a leaky faucet, a slow splatter from Harriet's Royal. From there it was mimeographed and mailed to 200 families—if, that is, we intended to keep the bulk rate. But the little church newsletter carried the names of the ages and all the feeling of fingers guided by a stubborn heart, determined to stay one beat ahead of life's final deadline.

6

Harold

Art of a Nonanxious Presence

So do not worry about tomorrow,
for tomorrow will bring worries of its own.
Matthew 6:34

In a world with the throttle pulled all the way out, Harold ran like an old tractor with a one-speed transmission. Harold's only speed was "slow." There was virtue to this settled-back style, but not virtue only. On good days, Harold crept along like a turtle, slow and steady, aiming at the finish line. On most days, he was inert as a possum hanging upside down, regarding this heels-over-head hysterical world with a studied indifference.

Harold Hatch was a house painter by trade—the best darned painter who was nonunion as a matter of sheer obstinacy. Probably, Harold was too slow at his work to flourish on union jobs. Just maybe, he was too exacting at it. Finally, he was less painter than artisan, born with the temperamental soul of a Michelangelo and much too inspired to be bothered with the vagaries of the trades—things like contractors, timetables, or the proverbial bottom line. He made very little money but was rich in stories, which he told all day long at the rate of about one per square foot of paint applied.

Harold was acquainted with the old techniques, now mostly lost and unaffordable at any rate—graining, feathering, shading, marbleizing. He had learned them from his father, who had painted himself silly in the insides of grand homes for the first families of Philadelphia. But Harold had arrived in our city like

39

some immigrant craftsman whose lifework is largely unrequired and unappreciated. He had started his own house painting business with what for him was a mountain of enthusiasm. This had soon waned. People paid too little and wanted work finished before it began. They had no concept of the careful art involved in true painting. And the help for hire couldn't aim paint at the side of a barn. After a two-year apprenticeship in futility, Harold had adopted in his work the wry disinterest most akin to his own deepest nature.

His wife of many years, Gladys, had attended our church for several years before Harold. There had been no good reason he could think of to waste a weekend morning in a pew, when bleachers, with or without a game, were more entertaining—not to mention the lure of a La-Z-Boy and the Sunday *Star.* He had joined the time-honored line of husbands, dropping their wives at the canopied drive, then whisking away to a full morning's freedom. This had suited Harold well, until the day he had been asked to paint the new church steeple.

While his wife had recommended his work to a trustee, Harold had accepted the assignment like some divine appointment. The steeple itself had been acquired from a wildly successful community church whose grandiose building plans had left it lying on the ground. Yet it was large enough that its place atop our little church was questionable at best. It was fashioned from ash wood and rose from an intricate octagonal base, resolving in a slender cone, and topped by a simple Latin cross. Harold was greatly taken by its details of craftsmanship, so rare on the jobs he generally found. Naturally, he took his sweet time, nursing the primer from roof ridge straight up, almost to heaven, it had seemed. Then back down and up all over again, twice with the finish coat. Finally, he added highlights on every angle in subtle polychrome until the whole thing shot out beams like the cross itself. Harold made it perfect "from ash to ash," as he put it, "like what they always say about people at funerals." Everyone who approached it on the County Line Road, as it grew to dominate their line of vision, acknowledged it to be the most magnificent steeple on a funny little church they had ever seen.

Meanwhile, as Harold had been teasing the rugged cross into loveliness, so it had been cajoling him to holiness. Maybe the roof had become his hermitage, a place too remote to converse with anyone but God. Or perhaps, as he faced the cross from heights each day, he began to see it looming large on the horizon of his own life. But by project's end, Harold was completely smitten by the cross and as much of its message as he could comprehend. For reasons far deeper than pride of accomplishment, Harold began to park the car on Sundays and accompany his wife into the little church with the giant steeple.

It soon became apparent to all that Harold could carry a tune, a near novelty among the congregational rank and file. He was asked and agreed to lead the modest adult choir, "For kicks and because I come cheap," as he liked to say. He sang and spoke a resonant bass, with that residual raspiness of a former smoker that readily commands attention. He directed the choir, however, as he did most everything else: minimally. His arms motioned only a casual interest in being heeded. Should the choir head off on its own during an anthem, that might be just as well. Most generally, he kept his index fingers waist high and thrust them forward and back like a pair of six-shooters. Sometimes, he would keep one hand at his side and shake the other one, palm up and limp at the wrist, as if he were Frank Sinatra turning to lead the pickup band through an interlude.

In due course, Harold had been courted for the position of church moderator, a role that befit him about as well as a gavel makes a suitable paintbrush. Yet, in a strange twist of irony, his devil-may-care demeanor made him the ideal candidate to moderate those discordant voices that took themselves more seriously even than Holy Scripture did. Business meetings were held on Wednesday evenings. Harold would arrive in painter's pants with scarcely a day's fleck of paint on them. Only his work shoes identified him as a painter—a fact answering to his habit of pausing in mid-stroke to converse at length with any fellow contractor, employer or passerby unwitting enough to strike up an innocent conversation on any topic of no consequence whatever. These shoes might have been swatches of canvas from a Jackson Pollock painting, their once-black leather a colorful chronology of every job Harold ever started and sometimes finished. They narrated a painter's progress, or regress, much the way layers of rock trace geophysical epochs.

Whenever the plague of rancor broke forth, Harold would saunter back a slothful step, the thumbs of his lacquer-thinnered hands looped over his waistband as if those six-shooters might be drawn at any moment. Then he would stare down the perpetrators in silence, his pupil points doing the talking, boring into them the pointlessness of carrying on any further. Never had matters been resolved so amicably among Baptists.

As the years passed, Harold became a champion of young pastors like myself, who came to serve the little church, green from seminary but flush with misplaced exuberance. He was a kind and calming influence on our early tutelage in ministry. He would patiently wait out the honeymoon, and when the first pastoral paint can fell off the ladder, Harold was there to help clean it all up. He would tell us of a young painter's dream and the trouble with a world severely lacking in imagination; and of the need to love life and all in it anyway, but not so much that it killed us; and how the greatest artisan was God, because he found how to make even the ugliness of the cross into a thing of sheer beauty. So, he would conclude, one should simply serve God, keep the paint on the canvas, and everything would work out more or less well.

Most of the time, that is what I have endeavored to do.

7

Billy

Forgiveness on a Wide Trajectory

A bruised reed he will not break. . . .
Isaiah 42:3

Billy played baseball—very well. He batted left and hit home runs over right field and into the woods with roughly the frequency that crows flew over church property to the next cornfield south.

Billy had been third baseman on the church slow-pitch softball team for a dozen years before he and his wife, Charlotte, finally darkened the church door on a regular basis. Congregational policy required players to attend worship at least one Sunday a month, but in Billy's case this would have been disastrous. Each Saturday from May to August the church's very reputation was on the line. Special dispensation was in order, so ballots had been cast. There were no negative votes, objections, or abstentions. Never before had the church constitution been spurned for the sake of a nonmember. But the fate of games and entire church league seasons hinged on the batting of Billy Burton. If anything at all was the gospel truth, surely it was this.

I played baseball—not very well.

Church league softball was my real pastoral audition. I had imagined that, after the Candidate Sunday sermon and the congregational vote, I was more or less "in." But softball games were never scheduled for the Sabbath. The congregation couldn't be faulted for that. Without a game to accompany my trial Sunday, there was no way to evaluate fairly just what order of

minister they had called. So the first softball Saturday of my
pastorate resembled the test drive of a newly purchased lawn-
mower. How does it run, corner, cut, field, and catch? These
were the questions that mattered.

I flew out, struck out, and singled, forcing an out at second.
At the bottom of every inning I was a lonely figure in the middle
of right field. Twice Billy's archnemesis from Grace Baptist, aptly
named Homer, launched balls over my head and into the woods,
as the crows taxied nervously nearby. Other than that it was
deader in right field than where the lawn tractor had cut the
grass too close to the ground in dry weather. The church flock
was less impressed even than the crows. It was as Billy always said:
"Let the preachers pray and the athletes play."

This was where things stood when Billy's only son, living at
home after a failed marriage, closed the garage door with the
car engine running and laid life's burden down on the backseat
of the family sedan. The day after the funeral, Billy had hung up
his baseball jersey on his suit coat hanger and found religion.
Every Sunday at 7:00 A.M. he tuned in to the gospel according to
televangelism to hear again the message he desperately craved:
that he, Billy Burton, was a miserable wretch of a man. Billy knew
why the TV preacher was shouting like that and at whom those
shouts were directed. He would have paid dearly for the sweet
solace of contrition stirred by that tireless tirade of incrimina-
tion. But early every Sunday it could be had on Channel 40 free
of charge. Then, dutifully, Billy would exchange sackcloth for a
suit and tie, drive to the church, drop a ten in the plate, and listen to an unbearable message of grace and forgiveness. The un-
welcome message was mine, and it struck Billy as no more than a
feeble attempt to undercut the artful discourse of a TV preacher
who already before breakfast had consigned Billy to eternal
perdition. It was an open-and-shut case. Justice had been served.

Never before had it dawned on me just what *bad news* the
Good News might appear to be.

It was not that Billy wasn't a miserable wretch. When it
comes right down to it, there is an ample degree of wretchedness
in us all. But quite apart from the naked truth about us, the
preaching of the church reveals the essential truth about God—
that God is gracious and willing and able always to forgive. If
anything was the gospel truth, surely it was this. But Billy would
have none of it.

Over the next months, I visited Billy and Charlotte several
times. Our conversations were often strained. Billy's sentences

circled like vultures around the subject of my preaching style. Then he would go in for the kill. He had a way of picking you apart that resembled the dissection of a frog. I am not sure he was aware of any real difference. At the heart of my Sunday message, something was missing for Billy. If I truly believed in divine judgment, then certainly I should be willing to say so in a loud voice, he reasoned. He couldn't quite tell just what it was I believed. But whatever it might be, what irked Billy the most was my habit, as I said it, of not screaming.

I, then, would raise the question of church baptism and membership. What, other than my preaching, might be standing in the way of his public declaration of faith?

Charlotte was already a Baptist but would not join the church without her husband's willingness to be baptized. Billy viewed this as an impossibility. He was too great a sinner. What if he were to emerge from the baptistery not only still a sinner but now also a hypocrite? The baptized must not sin. All the uncensored sanctimony of the airwaves Billy had taken in seemed to come down to this. After all the disappointment in his life, he had no intention of disappointing God. Billy was hell-bent on glimpsing grace from the back of right field.

Salvation came for Billy one day when his self-proclaimed saint of televangelism fell from grace. The one who condemned indiscriminately the faith experiences of practically everyone turned out in his sexual fetishes not to practice much discrimination at all. Shortly after the shocking news began to circulate, I went to Billy both to console him and to issue a challenge. Would he finally acknowledge that baptism was not our promise to God to be perfect and blameless, but our faith in God to be gracious and merciful? And I addressed him with a shout, reasoning that, if I truly believed in God's forgiveness, then certainly I should be willing to say so in a loud voice. Within three weeks of the death of false piety, Billy and Charlotte were down the aisle and into the loving arms of new life.

Never before had I experienced just what good news a piece of bad news might turn out to be.

Billy was baptized on a softball Saturday afternoon. He emerged from the water, threw on his jersey, and slugged three beauties deep into the woods, two of which have never been found. Sometimes, in the game of life, God bats left and hits one clean over the right field fence, while the crows scatter for cover.

8

Marie

Homecoming of an Articulate Heart

*For the message about the cross is foolishness to those who are
perishing, but to us who are being saved it is the power of God.*
I Corinthians 1:18

All things connect. People, places, and events form a twisted
thread of influence too thick to unravel or ignore. Marie was a
friend of a relative of an elderly couple of our congregation. She
lived in a large, stately home situated in a declining neighborhood, seventeen miles from the church. Hundreds of blocks of
winding city streets and a thousand churches of every stripe
and spot lay between her driveway and our parking lot. She had
held no church affiliation for over thirty years. Yet, for reasons I
have never fully understood, Marie chose our little church, out
on the county line, for her spiritual homecoming.

She was wheeled into worship one day, flanked by the elderly man, his wife, and her sister—Marie's dear friend. They
rolled her to the very front of the small sanctuary as heads
turned left and right, constrained to follow the rhythmic din of
one squeaky wheel. Marie wore oversized sunglasses and an even
bigger grin, and neither was removed for the entire hour. From
close range, she peered up at the pulpit, nodding intently at
points throughout the service, and when there arose the stray
chorus of "Amen," Marie chimed in with her own fervent and
mystifying "No!"

A stroke had left Marie paralyzed on one side and had
profoundly affected her speech. Her vocabulary was reduced to

a single word that had come to convey myriad thoughts and moods. That word—*Marie's word*—was "No!" As a child, I learned that *no* means no. For an eighty-five-year-old, sound of mind in every other way, *no* meant yes, no, and everything in between.

On my first visit to her home, I was ushered into a dimly lit room with curtains tightly pulled. Marie sat in her wheelchair on one side of a library table, displaying several scrapbooks and an old family Bible. The dark drabness of the setting was suffocating at first. I felt like Marie in sunglasses. As my eyes adjusted to available light, they were greeted by hundreds of other eyes, beaming out at me like stars on a planetarium ceiling, without beginning or end. Each wall was a gallery of old photographs, clumped into groups, as by family branch or generation. Marie's precious life and memory had been painstakingly preserved there for all to behold. Just then, her world was watching me.

One whole wall featured photos of a young Marie and a man who I later learned was her husband. The couple had been happily captured and framed in a dozen poses—on a Ferris wheel at the state fair, in a horse-drawn carriage, by the old state capitol, before the altar of God. . . . Her grinning face assumed a frown as she watched me watch her fondest past in pictures. She motioned me to her side. With scraps of former times and her gestures and "no's," I pieced together the fabric of Marie's charmed but tragic story. She and her husband were childless. He had been a successful merchant, but constant drink had hollowed him into a husk of a man. He lost a fortune and later his mind. During their last years together, he had grown increasingly violent. Finally, during one mad tirade, he had been forcefully removed to a sanitarium fifty miles to the north. Marie's first stroke had followed soon after, making visits nearly impossible, not that he would have known her. Still, she missed him terribly. Though he was resident in body only, the man she had loved, good and bad, still clung to her soul. As for other family and friends, there were few. Nearly all were casualties of time or forgetfulness, candles extinguished at the dusk of life. Marie was left alone in the dark.

She thumbed open her Bible at a frayed bookmark, tapped one crooked finger on the middle of the page, and uttered solemnly, "No, no-no-no!" My eye fell on a passage from Galatians, chapter 3. It read, ". . . for in Christ Jesus you are all children of God through faith. As many of you as were baptized into Christ have clothed yourselves with Christ." Marie wished to be baptized. She wished again to belong somewhere among the living.

The irony was clear to all. Our Baptist bylaws afforded virtually no exemptions to the immersion rule. The only proper mode of Christian baptism was, in a word, "wet." Before us was the grand exception to the rule—a paralyzed octogenarian with a one-word profession of faith. When asked if she wanted to consider her option to avoid the ritual altogether, she answered, predictably, "No, no!" Marie was bound and determined to experience these mystic waters for herself.

The deacons and I went to work on a logistical plan. The baptistery was accessed by way of a steep flight of stairs to the lip of the pool, then down several steps into the baptistery's center. Above the baptistery was a greatly enlarged photograph of a gently flowing stream at sunrise. Its bright orange hue ruled the chancel and drew the eye toward it in textbook Baptist fashion. The wrinkles and curled edges of this oversized wall poster were the evidence of frequent use. The humidity of a baptistery could reach hot-tub levels. To the sophisticated eye, it was gaudy to the point of embarrassment. But to a heart of simple faith, this was a scene of immense beauty. Many souls had died on this very spot, only to be raised to new life in the very next breath. Here resided the beauty of holiness.

On the appointed day, Marie arrived, squeaky wheel and all, at the door of the baptistery. She was dressed in a simple white gown. She and the gown were gingerly transferred to a stiff metal chair by two stout deacons. I prayed for the well-being of her mind, body, and spirit, and on no one present was this sentiment lost, as Marie prepared for the highest lift of her life since her Ferris wheel days. I climbed to the top and entered the baptistery. Marie and chair followed next, accompanied by three men and their grunts, with shirt sleeves in rolls and necks bulging until neckties resembled nooses. At the top, Marie was lowered warily into the water.

From her perch, suspended somewhere between life and death, Marie responded to a textbook catechetical inquiry with dispatch.

"Do you profess faith in Jesus Christ as Lord and Savior?"

"No, no, no!"

"Do you desire to be baptized?"

"No, no!"

"And do you, Marie, pledge to enter faithfully into the life of Christian service and love?"

"No, no, no, NO!"

Marie was visibly moved. The congregation shouted, "Amen!" Then, Marie was plunged, chair and all, into the waters of death. She came out grinning and whole, her eyes, minus the glasses, wide and knowing.

Faith in God boils down to a single, irreducible word. On rare occasions, in the lives of particular people, it achieves clearest expression. In heart and mind and grinning forbearance, Marie intoned that day the final affirmation. It is a cry from out of the darkness, as of Christ himself. The "no" of despair is extinguished by one blinding, earsplitting, unmistakable "yes!"

THREE

Sacred Spaces

The heavens are telling the glory of God;
and the firmament proclaims his handiwork.

Psalm 19:1

Every inch of earth is shot through with the holy,
and through the holes we steal a peek at heaven.

9

Sanctuary

Transcendence under a Low Ceiling

Do you know that you are God's temple,
and that God's Spirit dwells in you?
I Corinthians 3:16

Not all church sanctuaries are created equal. They come in countless styles, answering to the morass of period, place, and movement in which Christianity has flowered. I have always been partial to Gothic structures and their neo-Gothic counterparts because they seem somehow to participate in the mysteries to which they point. As a Baptist pastor, I have often lamented the premeditated disassociation with visible expressions of mystery, widely followed in Free Church traditions. In a visual age, worshipers locate their own sets of icons at any rate, from bad art, to shan-na-na singers, to a preacher's pompous hairdo. These tend understandably to reflect a more modern milieu. I find most all of them to be lightweight compared to those symbols that have borne the theological freight of the centuries.

The sanctuary of Ashgrove Baptist Church dated from the 1930s. It was a space of primary simplicity to which had been added a number of stock accouterments. Six double-hung windows supplied the sanctuary's only natural light. The stained glass in each bottom panel had been added mid-century. In color and texture, it called to mind the plastic color wheels of cardboard fireplaces that adorned living rooms at Christmas time throughout 1960s America. The carpet and pew cushions were deep red, so the thoughts of the gathered might not stray too far from the blood that flowed at Calvary. The plaster walls were painted white, purity on all sides, rising like doves from a red sea of redemption.

The raised chancel accommodated the standard pulpit, lectern, and Communion table, all in mission-style oak. In the apse rose the curtain of a baptistery, drawn open to display a large and unfortunate photograph of a stream at sunrise. Its yellow-orange hue and the sea of red all around it competed like opposing teams in bright-colored jerseys.

Topping it all were notably low-hanging rafters. They hovered at approximately the altitude of the ceiling in the new Wafflehouse restaurant down the road. This produced a suffocating effect, even taking into account our no-smoking policy. Low ceilings have been demonstrated to be emotionally and spiritually unhealthy. Psychological studies have linked lower ceilings to increased rates of suicide. Here was a hall that might drive a minister into a deep funk. Where would one encounter God in such a place? How might one touch the transcendent?

I determined to restore some holy mystery to the place myself. Certain options were already ruled out. The ceiling simply followed the contour of a modestly pitched roof. The stained glass and giant wall poster were gifts of a long-standing and still-standing member. The red pew cushions were relatively new and entirely too comfortable to be quibbled with. My attentions were settling elsewhere. The sanctuary was unusually wide for its depth, making the space virtually square in shape. Pews were arranged in two equal sections of fifteen rows each. Rows in each section were comprised of two smaller pew lengths pushed together. This brought the total number of pews to sixty. The whole configuration left three gaping aisles, while pushing pews to the very back wall. Standing at the pulpit on Sundays, staring, shouting, and even waving at the remote pews in which Baptists tend to congregate, I began to relocate chairs and churchgoers in my imagination. A whole host of new pew patterns began to suggest themselves. Soon I was building sanctuaries in the air.

On a particularly quiet Monday morning, I might have been spotted kneeling behind one of the benches like a good Catholic. Rather than for God or forgiveness, I was searching for any evidence of hardware used to secure a pew to concrete. There were no signs of screws, lug bolts, rivets, or fasteners of any kind. I grabbed hopefully to the rim of one pew back and attempted to tip it upward. Reluctantly, the runners tilted forward, revealing their deep imprint in the old, worn carpet. These pews were not nailed down. They had sat motionless for decades, captive only to their own stubborn weight. They could be freely rearranged into any configuration that space would accommodate and congregants would tolerate.

All that remained was to enlist a partner in crime, someone with tight lips and bulging biceps. I settled on one of the handful of teenage youth in the church, a strapping seventeen-year-old named Jed.

Jed Keltch attended the church with his mother, Pat, and a younger sister. Pat Keltch was a recent divorcee who had moved into an apartment complex at the county's edge. She had begun worshiping again as an expression of her resolve not to be undone by the reality of failure. Such a fixedness of purpose was less attainable for a teenager. Jed was by nature shy, and the transition to a new high school had been tenuous at best. His passion was football, and he was muscular beyond the dictates of chronological age. But he had not mustered the confidence to don pads and jersey and try out among strangers. He exhibited all the telltale signs of adolescent depression.

Jed had taken a shine to me. Perhaps it was my role as pastor, the fact that I was a male to be emulated. More likely, it was because I bragged on his sheer size compared to my own and fell into the habit of calling him "big guy." When I first approached him with my plan, Jed was a jumble of finger-biting nervousness. With a little effort, I convinced him that this would be an act sanctioned by proper authority. It was the truth. At a trustee board meeting, I had floated the idea of experimenting with the placement of church pews. A long silence had followed the suggestion. Finally, the board chairman had offered that this seemed fine with him, so long as I could find able bodies to carry it off. No one had volunteered. That is where we had left things, and where, no doubt, the trustees believed the pews were likely to stay as well.

Reluctantly, at first, Jed went along with my plan. But soon his spirit caught up with his body and began to lead the way. For several weeks in a row, we schlepped holy bleachers into various configurations. Late on Saturday afternoons, we would sneak into the church with burgers and fries and devour them irreverently on the sanctuary platform. As we washed them down, we would glance around, taking mental measurements. Then, for two hours or so, we would usher in a new era in sanctuary design.

Pews were arranged in the round and the half-round, at various angles turning inward, and facing each other in rows perpendicular to the platform, running north and south. We experimented with multiple rows, staggered rows, and the absence of rows altogether. Once, we even contemplated triangular clusters of pews, but this was abandoned on the basis that folks were too prone to cliquishness as it was.

Sunday followed Saturday, and with it arrived the predictable reactions of shock and intrigue. For starters, no one knew where to sit. Pew cushions, so accustomed over the years to certain posteriors that they literally held their shapes through the week, were now lost in a labyrinth of anonymity. Some people got in the habit of peeking into the sanctuary first and settling on a seat from a safe distance, so as to avoid wandering around in embarrassment. A few parishioners decided to keep away altogether until the whole madness played itself out. Most everyone who remained had a weekly opinion and found the inspiration to share it.

After several Sundays of this, the trustees had had enough. At half-past five o'clock on a Saturday afternoon, two of their number barged in, police-raid style, catching us in the act of assembling a bold semicircular design. They had intended to bring the whole thing to a screeching halt. Shocked to discover that it was only me and Pat's shy boy, Jed, they were stopped dead in their tracks. For several minutes they simply stared in disbelief, as the two of us panted and grunted our way toward our goal. Eventually, they could no longer help themselves and fell into place alongside us, even taking instructions. Thus refortified, we finished in record time and went out together to Dairy Queen. That Sunday the complaints continued, but two trustees remained uncharacteristically quiet.

The following Saturday, still others showed up and volunteered for service. They were armed as well—with their own views of how a house of God ought properly to be arranged. Week by week the numbers grew, until Jed and I were tripping over both feet and free advice. The whole enterprise was quickly losing its charm. Everything came to a head with a foolish suggestion that the pews be arranged in the shape of the cross. This required mental concentration turned to tedium by the chorus of opinions as to how a good cross should be fashioned.

The finished product was as ridiculous as the next Sabbath day's reactions to it.

"Make your cross and lie in it!"
"Put down your cross and have a seat!"
"Sit down, sit down *on* Jesus!"

Worst of all, an elderly worshiper's walker refused to fit between the pews at one of the cross's right angles. She took a spill and went down with speech as colorful as her undergarments. Morning worship was an amalgam of agony and hilarity. Someone summed up congregational sentiment with the suggestion that Christ had done the best job of lugging around the wood of the cross all by himself.

A congregational meeting was hastily called. I was accused of contributing to the delinquency of a minor. I pled guilty on the spot and sought forgiveness. It was granted, on the strength of Jed's newfound exuberance for practically everything. Over the previous month, the entire congregation and most especially his mother had watched with wonder. A new sense of place and purpose, surreptitious origins aside, seemed to have grown his enthusiasm for both worship and life in general. It had become almost as enormous as his upper body strength itself—but not quite.

A vote was taken to restore the pews to their original locations. A fund drive for new sanctuary carpet was begun. A motion to make it a nice blood red was unanimous. There was one abstention. Finally, it was settled by acclamation that, this time, the pews would be nailed down!

On the first Sunday back to worship in boring rows, Jed sat on the very front pew. When the song leader announced a congregational rendition of "Stand Up for Jesus, Ye Soldiers of the Cross," Jed was the first one to his feet. As our eyes met, he gave me a knowing sort of wink and then shrugged his shoulders as if to say, "Oh well, we gave it our best try!"

Watching him there, beneath a low sanctuary ceiling, I caught not even the faintest hint of adolescent depression. In its place was the very wonder and mystery of the faith I had sought. It had come to rest there, in that young, flesh-and-blood face of contentedness.

At one sitting, it was about all the transcendence I could stand.

10

Prayer Closet

Salutary Confinement

I called to the LORD out of my distress, and he answered me;
out of the belly of Sheol I cried, and you heard my voice.
Jonah 2:2

Within a month of my arrival at Ashgrove Church, I had memorized the names and faces of every parishioner. There was one exception, and it was not my fault: Millie Grimshaw and Effie Payne looked nearly identical. I could not tell them apart to save my life. My wife, Donna, who dissects faces in gruesome detail, informed me I was most grievously mistaken. Their eyes were set far out and close in, respectively; one nose hawked while the other one beaked; and their mouths were as dissimilar as smiles and frowns. Still, for my entire tenure as their pastor, I struggled to distinguish between them.

I was heartened one Sunday morning when Effie's own husband, Jake, came up behind Millie Grimshaw and tapped her on the shoulder. Jake and Effie were celebrating an anniversary, and Jake intended to surprise his wife with a little peck on the cheek. As Millie turned around, Jake beheld the mistaken object of his affections. He let out a loud snort. Millie let loose with a great gasp. Millie's husband, Sarge, who made it his business to observe everything, spit bullets. Jake was the closest thing Ashgrove Church had to a hopeless romantic. On this occasion, he had been a hopelessly hapless one.

"Of course, it might have been the similar length and color of their hair which threw him off," I suggested to Donna later.

"Effie's is bobbed and dyed red; Millie's is auburn and naturally curls under," she corrected.

Even without Donna's assistance, I had already come to a firm conclusion: there are subtle forces at work in and around us that contribute to our apprehension of things. They are non-quantifiable. In the interpersonal arena, between skins, these are known as vibes, chemistry, magnetism, natural affinity, and the like. In the intrapersonal realm, within our own skins, we have named them intuitions, premonitions, a sixth sense, and sometimes even the presence of the holy or the voice of God.

To this day I am certain of it. A force exists that binds Effie and Millie in a peculiar way, though of this they appear to be utterly unaware. And for some reason, equally shrouded in mystery, I have been granted the eyes to see it.

While it took four whole weeks and immense concentration to greet the Ashgrove flock without feeling sheepish, I had memorized the church's floor plan on my very first day. It was an uncomplicated layout. In truth, it had been a bit of a disappointment. All older buildings have something to hide. It might be a room that is smaller than exterior dimensions would suggest, a set of stairs that no longer reach their destination, or a threshold that once led somewhere but has been filled in and covered over like ground above a grave. It might even be a hidden panel or a crawl space containing a box of old photos or letters from long ago days. The particulars are unimportant, but the principle is universal. Old buildings harbor secrets that they are willing to tell. It is as inescapable as the skeletons in everyone's closet, which will always find a way to rattle sooner or later. The fact that Ashgrove Church seemed to be the sole exception to this rule was greatly disheartening. I had begun to feel swindled.

Then had come the first baptism of my pastorate. Pat Keltch's son, Jed, my partner in the sanctuary pew caper, made the profession of faith in Christ, and I braved the steep heights of the Ashgrove baptistery for the first time. I had rehearsed the sharp ascent like a climber training to scale Everest. Deacons would be watching, I had surmised. I had no intention of embarrassing myself. That was when I had finally noticed it. Behind the steep flight of stairs, cut into the wall beneath the baptistery itself, was a short, four-paneled door. Its top edge was cut at a steep angle to conform to the underframing of the baptistery. The door had a rusty rimlock, but the knob was broken off. Here, at long last, was a case for the budding architectural archeologist.

On the Monday after baptism Sunday, I nearly raced through the sanctuary and behind the chancel to the baptistery. I tried to bare hand the stem of the rimlock, but its spring mechanism was stiff and ungiving. Clearly, the door hadn't been opened in years.

As I considered how to gain entry, Russ Ingersol, church custodian, appeared on cue, just as it seemed he always did.

"Got some pliers?" I asked.

Between Russ's vise grips and my WD-40, the rimlock finally loosened up and began to turn.

"What's this room ever been used for, Russ?" I inquired.

"Don't know, quite, Preacher. Not much I'd say. Least not since we got city water and all the baptistery plumbing got run out this side." Russ was pointing to the back of the baptistery, where copper piping and a drain line exited to the west.

"Never even been in there myself," Russ added.

Finally, the gears of the lock moved freely, and the stem easily turned. Following some adrenaline-pumping squeaks and creaks, the secret door was open. The space was pitch black. Russ rounded up a flashlight, and we aimed the beam around the room. The walls were just exposed studs and laths, and the ceiling was no more than six feet tall. The air was musty and dank, presumably from the condensation of baptismal water— holy drippings on unwashed ground. Cobwebs abounded. Unremarkable artifacts littered the grimy floor: short sections of copper pipe and bits of solder, an old box of candles, several mildewed cardboard fans with picturesque scenes of far-away places. An old pair of waders hung on a nail at the far end of the closet.

But my eyes had gravitated to the center of the small space. There, covered in dust, were a plain, wooden writing desk and chair. A single, broad-based candleholder sat on the desktop. The desk's only drawer was slightly ajar. Firmly, I pulled it open while Russ shined the light. Inside were three books: a leather-bound King James Bible, a copy of Broadman's *The American Hymnal*, from 1926, and a handsome edition of Thomas à Kempis's *The Imitation of Christ*. Inside the front cover of this last book was scrawled a name. The script was faint and florid, but with effort I forced what appeared as random letters into my own gestalt.

"Emil Bushnell," I read.

"Oh, sure!" said Russ. "Second guy out there on the preachers' wall. Was preacher when they moved the church out, I think."

"But, why would he have left his things in here?" I wondered aloud.

"Don't know," Russ said. "Might ask Millie. She was a kid, but I bet she'd remember."

"Millie. That's Jake's wife," I declared timidly.

"No. Millie's Sarge's wife. Effie's Jake's wife."

"Right!" I said.

From what Millie knew and what I could piece together from old church records, a story began to take shape—with my own creative filler, of course. Back in the 1930s, Emil Bushnell had presided over the move out to the county line. He was a second-generation German immigrant, who had been educated back East. He had come to the downtown church in 1931, hoping to see it grow into a flagship congregation. But the parcel of land on which the church sat had been annexed for the expansion of a state college. The church had been forcibly displaced. Bushnell had dutifully followed his flock out to the little grove on the county's western edge, but he had done so with great reluctance. Emil Bushnell had been bred in the city. Pastoring in the cornfields had been tantamount to missionizing aboriginals on some distant soil. Still, he had persevered.

"A soul mate!" I told myself.

There were still missing pieces. Why had he kept the desk in the closet? And what had become of him? His name simply disappeared from the records halfway through the year 1939.

"Don't rightly know," Millie said. "Might ask Old Man Norris. He's been here longer than anybody. If anybody knows, bet he does! 'Member though—talk loud! Merle's deafer'n a ear a' corn!"

Merle Norris remembered well—or as well as a ninety-four-year-old remembers anything.

"Yeah. Ol' Bush, as they called him. Didn't like that though, I recall. We hardly baptized a soul in those days. But Bushnell took a likin' to that spot for some reason 'er 'tother. He'd go in there and light his candles and read and pray. Some took to callin' him 'Jonah in the whale,' down there underneath the baptistery and all. He didn't last long, though. One day he just up and died. They say the country killed him. S'pose anything's possible...."

Old Man Norris had sounded skeptical. Of course, he had good reason to believe people were supposed to live forever.

Back at the closet, I sat down in Emil's chair to think.

Outside the room were a small vacuum cleaner and a utility light. I had planned to illuminate the space and give it a thorough sprucing up. Instead, I was hunkered down like a noncombatant in a bomb shelter.

I was just beginning to appreciate what had drawn Bushnell to the spot. Something was here—down in the belly of the whale, beneath the baptismal waters of chaos. There was an enchantment to this site, which, long ago, Emil Bushnell had come to feel and to which he, himself, had contributed. Here he had met the living God, I concluded, and that encounter had sustained him.

There exist places that are, in a word, holy. Maybe this is explained by the great fervor of those who have sojourned on those spots. Perhaps certain souls have marked them like a trail with the very blood and sweat of their own faithful struggles. Or perhaps it is simply that God has chosen to be especially present in them. But the essence of such places is much like that of people. Finally, they remain inscrutable, forever enshrined in deep and unfathomable mystery. Somehow, the lives of Millie and Effie were ineffably linked, though even face-to-face they never perceived it. Emil Bushnell's life span and mine were separated by a score of years, yet I had become intensely aware of a palpable bond between us. And while our connection seemed to arise from a shared struggle to find our places in the church, it had been the unlikely rediscovery of a forgotten place in that same church that had brought this bond to consciousness.

I untangled the extension cord and hung the trouble light on a nail. I was about to turn it on when something stopped me. It was almost like a hand reaching out to hold me back, yet it had come, not from spaces beyond, but from a place deep within. In five minutes, I returned from the kitchen with a matchbook. After placing one of Emil's two remaining tapers in the candlestick, I struck a match and lit it. Closing the door of the closet, I commenced with an act which, over the course of a pastorate, I would often repeat. I sat at the desk of Emil Bushnell, folded my hands, and prayed.

11

The Peanut Gallery
Outliving Our Youthfulness

They shall ask the way to Zion, with faces turned toward it,
and they shall come and join themselves to the Lord
by an everlasting covenant that will never be forgotten.
Jeremiah 50:5

Along the west wall, just outside the sanctuary of the Ashgrove Baptist Church, stretching southward into the fellowship hall, is a series of black-and-white photographs. They hang at eye level so passersby can clearly glimpse the faces of those portrayed there. It is also, I suspect, so the pictured can easily stare back at those who have turned aside to pay them regard. It is the gallery of former pastors, aptly if ironically referred to as the "preachers' peanut gallery."

I have always been leery of "hanging" portraits. At the National Portrait Gallery in London there hangs a rendering of my ancestor, Sir Thomas Wyatt "the Rebel." His father, Sir Thomas Wyatt "the Poet," my namesake, is remembered for introducing the Petrarchan sonnet into English verse. A thoroughgoing romantic, he was the childhood sweetheart of Anne Boleyn. Anne, of course, went on to bigger things, becoming the second wife of Henry VIII, and later the beheaded wife of Henry VIII, making room for his third bride, Jane Seymour. It was out of this debauchery that Henry separated England from Rome and fathered Anglicanism, unleashing a dispute on British soil that endures to this day.

Sir Thomas Wyatt the Rebel led the failed insurrection against Mary Tudor, "Bloody Mary," the daughter of Henry's first wife, Catherine of Aragon. When she ascended the throne in 1553, Mary busied herself with the task of restoring Roman Catholicism to the realm and began burning her detractors at the stake under the reenacted religious heresy laws. After a good bit of this, Sir Thomas Wyatt the Rebel lost his head— figuratively and literally. The painting of him in question is a neck-up portrait. The docent described this as an ironic commentary on the nature of his demise. Tourists around me chuckled. I alone was gagging. I turned off from the tour and sat down to sulk. A few hundred years may have passed, but family is still family.

Ever since learning of the gruesome slaying of my direct ancestor and its humiliating public reminder on daily display, I have winced at the idea of personal portraits—not that anyone has ever asked me to sit for one. But how different, really, was a poster-size photograph? I well understand that we live in the land to which our Baptist forbears fled from tyranny in England, this free land that they went on to help shape, championing the Bill of Rights and the antiestablishment clause of the Constitution. That very same freedom provided the safe underlay for the congregational story, which collectively, these photographs portrayed. But none of this has mediated my distaste for the idea of my own image hanging in perpetuity behind glare-free glass.

"Is someone going to hang *me* up here?" I asked Harold Hatch, church moderator.

"Not until you leave," he said, "or die. . . ."

"Good!" I said. "I think. . . ."

This did, in fact, bring some immediate relief, on the order of, say, Alka-Seltzer. But my stomach began to churn all over again as I pictured myself in the year 2098, staring out from that wall at little children or young teens peering up at me, betraying the natural apprehension of the young for the ancient, or giggling at my beady eyes and mushed nose and stupid tie, while I could only continue to smile back in witless congeniality. It was then that I determined to learn what I could about the men of the peanut gallery, whose chiseled faces once posed for the camera, entrusting their images to an unknown future.

Six photographs lined the wall. A seventh frame held the figure of cross, anchor, and crown, ancient symbol of the church, this in lieu of a photograph of the organizer of the original downtown Sunday school. It was captioned simply, *Horace Green, 1917.* The remaining frames carried small brass plates engraved with names and years of pastoral service. I scoured the scant church record for any mention of them and picked through the recollections of old-time members. Soon the photos began to come to life like muscle and sinew over skeletal remains in Ezekiel's vision of the dry bones.

Carlisle West—1918–1926, a West Virginian, moved the little mission out of its beer-garden surroundings to a plain frame chapel. The church was undoubtedly chartered at that time, but no founding records are extant. They fell victim, no doubt, to that fateful broom of spring cleaning, by whose bristles so much of what has been is now lost to all but the mind of God. West seems to have been a tireless crusader for the Christian cause. He began actively to missionize the neighborhoods of Haughville, the western suburb of Indianapolis, where simple but hardy stockyard and factory workers sought a better life. They came with unlettered zeal, establishing early on the common but incorruptible character that has marked the church's life ever since.

Wilkes Cobb—1927–1932, was cut from different cloth. He hailed from the New Hampshire uplands, in the heart of the great granite state. His face itself appeared set in granite, as if resisting what little if any allure the land of Indiana limestone might have held for him. Cobb gained a reputation as the plodding pulpiteer, who took his erudite time spinning out a gospel word. Unfortunately, the attention spans of the faithful were limited. No one had been able or willing to wait him out to the end. Hearers were like poor souls, dropped in the ocean deep and finally drowning just twenty-five feet from the blissful shore. Cobb's pastorate was like his preaching, only inverted. He had wearied inwardly, longing for the distant shores of New England. After four and a half unproductive years, Cobb had left Indianapolis and returned to the East, where he served churches and lived out his days in relative bliss.

Emil Bushnell—1933–1939, whose story I had already unearthed with the discovery of the prayer closet beneath the baptistery, had literally given his life to the congregation's resettlement in the little grove on the county line. Emil and I were soul mates in absentia. I was never entirely certain what this meant, but the sheer fact of it drew me almost daily to the curious closet of prayer behind the Ashgrove chancel.

George Adbury—1940–1961, through his long tenure, was largely responsible for the "countrifying" of the congregation, steadily replacing its urban, blue-collar base with the working class of rural Indiana. Nearly every congregational history features some beloved servant of God, a pastor for the ages whose memory ferments like a fine wine over time into the stuff of legend. At Ashgrove, this pastor was George Adbury. It was recalled that every day he wore a vest and tie over a white starched shirt with the sleeves rolled up high like a common field hand. Atop a thick head of hair and accompanying him wherever he went was a brimmed hat. It was said he took it off only to preach. There was no sign of it in the photograph, but I was certain I could make out the hat line and distinguish the slightly matted hair above it. Tabulating recollections of Adbury's activity left the distinct impression that he was always in his study, in everyone's home, and at the county hospital or the mortuary, at one and the same time. Either he worked himself silly, hired a double, or was actually twins. On the other hand, it is possible he simply had that special knack for being where he was needed when he was needed—a gift, I have concluded, that puts us at ease because it reminds us of God's gracious ubiquity, which is of course the only Presence in life or death we can ever really count on anyway. When a pastor's presence brings reassurance of that, he or she is greatly rewarded by the amiable thoughts of others.

During Adbury's pastorate, the church reached its peak membership of 265 persons, a veritable megachurch considering the population's sparseness out on the county's edge. Undoubtedly, he was the single most important reason the Ashgrove Church survived at all. Adbury was the only pastor to retire from Ashgrove. He and his wife, Clara, moved to Roanoke, Virginia, her birthplace, and lived out some peaceful years together. He gave up starch and vests, it was said, but he died with his hat on.

Roy Shales—1963–1967, had awaited Adbury's day of departure like a buzzard circling for a good feed. Roy hailed from Preachersville, Kentucky, a rut in the road running by the Dix River, thirty miles south of Lexington. He and his wife, Lydia, had matriculated to Indianapolis in the mid-fifties and settled on a small wooded acreage west of the church, near the tiny town of Nebo. This, Roy had begun systematically to clear, while he

worked odd jobs for local farmers and farm implement sup-
pliers. Lydia supplemented the family income handsomely,
quickly gaining the reputation as an able seamstress for hire. It
was she who later had proposed to the Ashgrove quilters that
they begin to sell their work for a fat price. The quilters had
dismissed the suggestion for reasons of deep conviction they
could never quite put into words.

But Roy had ambitions. A lifelong Baptist, he claimed to
have attended a Bible college in eastern Kentucky and to have
earned a doctorate by mail. Roy had begun to "circuit ride" the
small county churches, preaching on Sunday nights, conducting
revival days and the like. Several members of Ashgrove had
attended one or more of these events and were impressed with
Roy's oratory.

Not long after George Adbury's retirement, the elderly
interim minister had grown gravely ill, and the pulpit had fallen
vacant. Upon strong recommendation, Shales had been invited
by the deacons to supply preach and, as is so often the way in
these matters, one thing led to another.

By early in the year 1963, Shales had killed the search process and been voted in as Ashgrove's pastor. For a year or two, the
congregation was reasonably pleased. Roy brought a natural
energy and a passion to all he did. But in time, that quality of
presence, so integral to the ministry of George Adbury, became
contrasted by Roy's ministry of "absence." When Roy was not in
the pulpit, which of course was most of the time, he could most
generally be found in his woodpile, chopping logs to splinters.
More and more of his attentions had been devoted to his firewood business on the side. He claimed that he wrote his best
sermons as he chopped, but since none had heard Roy preach
but one message over and over again for a very long time, suspicions had persisted. The fact that he preached peripatetically,
ranting and raving as far afield from the text as his legs carried
him from the pulpit, did not strengthen his case with the congregants. It became ever more clear with the passage of time that
Roy Shales was an ersatz pastor but a firewood dealer in earnest.
Simply put, Roy was a man of distraction. He could neither stand
nor sit still.

Meanwhile, Roy had been draining the church dry as a
cofferdam. When it was discovered that he had been investing in
wood-chipping machines, suspicions turned to accusations. By
then, Roy had taken his business public and was already selling

stove lengths and wood chips in four counties. He was employing a team of five full-time wood choppers and tree trimmers
and wisely resigned his Ashgrove post before the deacons could
get up the nerve to fire him. Unfortunately, most every church
history includes at least one example of this manner of recollection. The photo of Roy Shales still hangs on the wall of the peanut gallery, a visual call to vigilance in the face of that sometimes
fine line between ardent zeal and artful deceit.

   Milton Hawkes—1968–1985, my predecessor, had come to
the rescue of the church and settled in for a long pastoral
tenure. Milton's was a bivocational charge from the outset.
Though ordained within the denomination, he was a career
substitute with the Hendricks County consolidated school system. He favored the fourth and fifth grades but filled in wherever he was needed for nine months of the year. Twice the
church endeavored to persuade him to abandon teaching and
become their full-time pastor. Ed Garrett, enterprising Ashgrove
trustee, had gone so far as to draw up a challenge budget to that
effect, but Milton had resisted. Both he and the congregation
knew that they could not muster the resources to support him
and his family of five. And while he enjoyed the pulpit, his
passion had always been the classroom. Finally, Milton had been
cajoled out of limbo the other way, accepting a position as an
elementary school vice principal on the far side of the county.
At the summer's close in 1985, he and his wife, April, had bid the
church in the grove a tender farewell.

   In its years with Milton Hawkes, the Ashgrove congregation
had grown both more independent of pastoral leadership in its
daily affairs and more neglectful of its long-term purpose and
mission beyond church walls. My close scrutiny of the peanut
gallery had helped me understand Ashgrove's checkerboard
history as the real ground of ministry on which I might build.
The ministry itself, I was learning, was more involved than a
game of checkers. It featured complicated players, stealth moves,
and surprises at every turn. It was much more like a game of
chess . . . and I hate chess.

   But the peanut gallery had left me chastened besides. Only
two of Ashgrove's former pastors were yet alive: Milton Hawkes
and Roy Shales—if, that is, no one had yet slowed Roy down long
enough to throttle him. These pictures had hung there long
before I arrived, and they would be hanging long after I was
gone. It all boiled down to that cardinal lesson of Adbury's

pastorate, to the message of the gospel itself: we are each expendable. And this is a good thing, because we are each temporary as well. The real purpose of our individual ministries, bound as they are by finitude, is to reflect the eternal, to elucidate the reliable presence of Christ, to point up the gracious permanence and the permanent graciousness of the Living God.

As I prepared to leave the pastorate at Ashgrove Baptist Church, I revisited with my dear friend Harold Hatch the whole matter of the peanut gallery and my participation in its commemorative intent. I had been the seventh pastor in the church's history—the biblical number of completion in a long and illustrious line of leadership. It seemed to me, I had suggested, that every seventh pastorate ought to be represented as was the first, the unknown *Horace Green*—with the cross, anchor, and crown, symbols of Christ's ubiquitous, eternal presence. What did Harold think of that, I wanted to know.

"In a pig's eye!" he said.

The next time I visit Ashgrove Church, I'm thinking, I may sneak in such a picture and plaster it over my own sorry image, just to see if anyone notices. Either that, or I'll employ a permanent marker and make some favorable changes to my eyes, nose, and stupid tie—changes that, with any luck, will long outlast me.

12

Locks and Keys

Blaming the Victim

. . . and the doors of the house where the disciples had met
were locked for fear of the Jews. Jesus came and stood among
them and said, "Peace be with you."
John 20:19

For the first thirty years of the church's existence, the doors
to Ashgrove Baptist Church were never locked. Members came
and went at will, like bees buzzing around a hive. The chance
traveler could stop in for a moment's reprieve from the heat of
the day, take repose in the holy hush of the sanctuary, or even
nose around for a glass of water. A plaque hung above the
church door as if to countenance the policy. It read, *Come unto*
me, all ye that labour and are heavy laden, and I will give you rest.

A small offering box had been placed in the vestibule, and
each Sunday morning it was ceremoniously opened by a deacon.
While generally the box was empty, over the years some remarkable stories of its contents had accrued and been duly incorpo-
rated into the church's collective memory: a twenty-dollar bill
with a note attached reading, simply, "Thank you!"; seventeen
pennies along with a child's picture of a smiley face; a message
scrawled on the back of a gum wrapper—"I took a Bible. Will
pay you back soon! God bless you!" Even the occasional Ben
Franklin or U.S. Grant had been left, with positively no explanation at all.

The most celebrated account, told every initiate at least
once by Herb Chestnut, the deacons' chairman, concerned a

75

message he himself had discovered the Sunday before Christmas in 1969. "I found God in your church today. I'm giving these up. Thank you for being here when I needed you! Merry Christmas! I love you all!" Below the note were seven suspicious-looking pills, which IPD narcotics experts determined to be mescaline, a psychedelic drug derived from the stems of a Mexican cactus.

"Well, *Felice Navidad!*" Harold Hatch had exclaimed.

By then, the open-door policy was already in jeopardy. The tentacles of the sprawling city had finally reached the edge of the little grove and cut their own path to the door for a mischievous look around. The first signs of trouble were imprinted on tin cans—specifically the colorful logos of Hamm's, Budweiser, and Pabst Blue Ribbon. They were scattered here and there, and occasionally shot through with the kind of holes a .22-caliber rifle makes. Now and again, the charred wood of a bonfire was found by the copse of trees on the east fringe of the property. Once, near midnight, Winslow Cox had spotted such a blaze from out on the road. Without hesitation, he had driven his truck right up to the pyre, training his brights on the scene like a Coast Guard cutter. Six adolescents, male and female, had stumbled to their feet, blinded by the beam. They were teens the age of Win's own sons, but he didn't recognize the first one of them.

"Get outta here, now!" he had shouted. "No burnin' on this property! You all get on home!" With a fidgety defiance, they had stomped off across a field to destinations untold, as Winslow grabbed a shovel from his truck bed and proceeded to bury their light under a bushel of black dirt.

Yet trouble on the property continued to pop up like crabgrass. Graffiti was spray painted on the side of the church. The deep tire tread marks of many a muddy joy ride were left in the lawn. Most heinous was the occasional used condom, lying limp on the drive as if in scorn of all pious sensibility. The deacons fell into the habit of arriving before the first worshipers on Sunday, in order to remove any sight unsuited to the eyes of the gentler sex.

It was only a short while later that this walk on the wild side finally strolled into the unbarred building. First, small objects turned up missing—a small wall clock, a Communion cup, a brass cross. Minor vandalism followed. Hymnbooks were thrown on the floor and chairs were overturned. A wall mirror was cracked and the refrigerator raided. But when Warner Sallman's sweet rendering of Jesus got handlebars and glasses, people began to get restless. The deacons and trustees met together to consider a modification of their long-standing policy. On one side of the door was the venerable practice of openness. The church ought to bar no one from entry. The church door was but a threshold to the field of mission, nothing more, nothing less.

On the other side was common sense. How many folks still turned down their beds at night with their doors unlocked or even left them open during the day? Even out in the bullheaded boondocks, the practice was increasingly rare. The world was changing, and sensible people had to adapt along with it. The stewards of the church had an obligation to protect both people and property from those elements wishing to inflict harm. To lock or not to lock? To bar or forebear? The matter was brought to congregational vote. In a squeaker, the hinge had closed shut. A locksmith was hired. Keys were issued reluctantly at first, but over time, every man, woman, child, and friend of the church who wanted a key had received one.

When I began my pastorate at Ashgrove Church, the front door had been locked for a dozen years. Jesus' words in Matthew had been taken down from above the front entrance for repainting and then lost or misplaced. The donation box was now stenciled over with the word "Suggestions." One needed a crowbar to pry open even the slightest memory of the days preceding locks and keys. Yet, shortly after I had first arrived, free access pushed again into the forefront of everyone's mind.

A copy machine in the provisional church office was stolen. There was no sign of forced entry. No windows were broken, locks pried loose, or doors left ajar. Gladys Hatch had reported that Church Mutual Insurance was willing to reimburse but was concerned that the theft appeared to have been perpetrated in-house. Naturally, the standard $200 deductible on loss of contents would apply. Harriet Crabtree, publisher of the little weekly church letter, *The Link*, had been forced to resurrect the old mimeograph machine. About this, Harriet showed not the first sign of perturbation. She had resisted the purchase of the copier in the first place. Harriet harbored the same suspicion toward the Xeroxing of her words that some religionists have about the photographic copying of their own image. Privately, Roy Higgins, the deacon vice chairman, had compared her to an old dog who can't learn new tricks. For Harriet herself, the subject seemed to strike at something deep and inexplicable within her.

A fresh debate about locks and keys had ensued. The trustees estimated that no fewer than seventy-five persons had a church key. Many were nonmembers and had not passed through the doors of the church for months or even years—at least not by the light of day.

The deacons' concern was for congregational esprit de corps. Was there a klepto in the church? Who could it be? Would God's people begin to turn a suspecting eye toward one other?

"What about the young people in the church?" Herb had heard a woman conjecture. "Who's that new boy—Patricia Kletch's son, Jed? Who knows anything about him?"

"Well, between you and me, I don't know how Cynthia Green 'n' her three get by on that little job a' hers down there at the dollar store," someone else had commented. "I know their daddy don't support."

All the leadership was agreed that it was time to rekey the locks. This go-round, they would do things right. Kip Quarfarth's brother-in-law was a locksmith, and he was prepared to do the job for cost. The trustees would make up a sign-out sheet for anyone issued a key. Only church officers and those with legitimate cause would get one. It was suggested that a lock be installed on the office door as well.

"Not everybody on earth needs in there fer mercy's sake!" Sarge had put it.

"What about the sanctuary?" someone else had wondered. "And how 'bout the preacher's office?"

"Well," said Sarge, suddenly casting a censorious eye in the direction of my silence, "so whatty 'bout it, Pastor? What you think 'bout all this?" I told them I was not at all certain what to think. No ready biblical reference came to mind. But I did recall the story of the cash register in my grandfather's drugstore in Monette, Arkansas. Monette was a small town of one thousand not-so-well-off people. About twice a year, someone or other would get up the courage to break into his store and take whatever was there for the taking. My grandfather's cash register sat on a counter near the very middle of the pharmacy. It was a jewel of an antique, built of thick hardwood and trimmed in solid brass. A bell rang with authority throughout the store every time the change key was struck.

Grandfather prized it above any other piece of equipment in the place—more than the adding machine or the watch case or calendar wall clock or the even the elaborate soda fountain.

Once only had he locked the register on the night of a burglary. On that occasion it had been jimmied open with such force that the whole front of the cash drawer lay in pieces on the floor. But Grandfather was not in the habit of repeating mistakes. Sometimes the case is more valuable than the contents. Any cash left in the register was small potatoes compared to its intrinsic, sentimental worth. And anyone determined enough to break in the building would find a way into the cash box anyway. Once repaired, the drawer was left open after hours. At closing time, the last sound one would hear was Grandfather's finger on the change key, and the bell resonantly ringing in the dusk.

With my story out of the way, the deacons and trustees commenced with their plan. The outside door locks were refitted, and twenty new keys issued, including mine and the custodian's. A new lock was placed on the office door, though Harriet thought this foolish. Only five office keys were dispensed. I opted not to have a lock on the door of my study, and the deacons and I concurred that all keys to the sanctuary should remain in the hands of Christ.

Fresh complaints surfaced almost immediately. Sunday school teachers, who had not been issued keys, felt slighted. They pointed out that while they taught in the church every Sunday, some church officers sat on their hands until a board meeting came up. Hassie Longstreet had agreed to let the quilters in the building on Tuesdays, but she routinely forgot. And Winslow Cox, who lived closer than anyone else to the church, was getting calls at all hours of the day and night from those needing immediate access to the building. Harold Hatch had predicted just such a turn of the tide, but the leaders were determined to stay the course.

Before long, a new gale blew across the bow. On All Saint's Day, the Sunday following Halloween, I arrived to a great commotion on the north lawn of the church. A sanctuary window had been smashed to flinders and then cleared out of glass from top to bottom. A large storage trunk lay on its side, several feet from the church. A dozen worshipers were hovered over it, as if it were the corpse of a fallen saint. It had been lifted through the window and dragged to the spot. In the trunk had been stored old records and papers of the church, sheathed and bound in brown filing envelopes. Collectively, they comprised a church's equivalent to the epochal record made by layers of soil in the earth. They went all the way down—downtown, that is—to its

inner-city origins in a German beer garden. Just then, history
was turned on its side, where it had been unceremoniously
excavated. Two hundred plus pounds of heritage had been
dragged across the ground until the thieves had thought to
examine their treasure before offering any more of the muscle
of indenture. After mangling the lock, they had discovered no
assets more liquid than a slight trickle of history.

In the church itself, the news was nearly as favorable. The
door to the provisional office had been pried open, but the
mimeograph machine was intact. It sat confidently in its place
and said nothing. It was like Harriet herself when she was right
about something and you and she both knew it, as, through the
thick silence, her every fiber communicated softly and simply,
"You see! . . ." Indeed, nothing at all in the whole space had
been touched or taken. The same was true of my study. Every
book, from leather-bound Bibles to pricey commentaries, stood
unmolested on its shelf. Only a paperweight was missing. It had
been a gift. Affixed to a marble base had been two intersecting
golf clubs with a golf ball in between. To a nongolfer, it had
seemed to indicate either poor judgment or wishful thinking. I
was not in the least teed off by its loss. Clearly, the perpetrators
found no value in the tools of the work of God. No objects of any
clear value were missing. But the office door was hacked to
splinters. It and the window had to be replaced. Church Mutual
paid in full, after subtracting the standard $200 deductible, of
course. I heard in my mind the sound of grandfather's old cash
register, ringing open to remove the bills. . . .

In the aftermath, a church divided remained so. Some
spoke of installing iron bars over the windows. Others simply
wanted their old keys back. Meanwhile, the resolve of deacons
and trustees had been filed down to shavings. The quilters and
Sunday school teachers soon received new keys. Before long,
nearly everyone else had gotten them as well. About half the
time, the last one out the front door forgot to lock it anyway. On
no other occasion during my tenure did anyone pilfer the
church. Probably, word got around that there was nothing there
worth bothering with. The plaque bearing the Scripture from
Matthew was repainted and hung once more above the church
door. It had been found in the corner closet behind the chancel,
on the spot from which the trunk of records had been dragged.
It adorns the entrance still, a reminder of old that the rest and
peace of Christ can be given but not taken, shared but not
stolen. They are God's simple gifts, gifts beyond price.

13

Pet Cemetery
Hallowed Ground

For every wild animal of the forest is mine,
the cattle on a thousand hills.
I know all the birds of the air,
and all that moves in the field is mine.
If I were hungry, I would not tell you,
for the world and all that is in it is mine.
Psalm 50:10–12

Down the road from the Ashgrove Baptist Church, sitting contentedly on the slight crest of a hill, is an 1860s Quaker meeting house. On a vast prairie, it occupies the only raised earth in sight. It is as if the founders spied out higher ground and claimed it outright, there being no one else around to dispute the matter. Immediately behind the building is a churchyard, fenced in wrought iron. It is rectilinear in shape, containing several long, regular rows of graves.

A few trees, mostly locust and elm, intersperse the mosscovered monuments. Names, once deeply etched in stone, have worn away through rain-soaked time—appellations now mingled with the bones who bore them. Dates still decipherable have their own tales to tell. Many are tragic, little lives lost to unknown cause. Was it smallpox or yellow fever, tuberculosis or influenza? There are dates of birth and death from the same year, or month, or day—stories as short as the hyphens between them. There are markers harboring the faded names of siblings,

stricken together. Their hidden narratives are far too grievous to
unearth at any rate.

On occasion, for its sheer quickening power, I would visit
the spot, referred to by some as the "friends of the Friends
yard." But as I walked its rows in the still, hot summer air, a
different phrase burned in my mind. "Hallowed," is what came
to rest there—sanctified, blessed, consecrated ground.

Ashgrove Church came late to the practice of cloistering the
dead on church property. Long before they moved to the grove
of maple and ash out on the county line, church members laid
their own to rest in family plots around the city and state and as
deep into the South as a mortuary would deliver. When earth
was first turned for the hallowed dead of Ashgrove, the dearly
departed were not the grandmas and grandpas, uncles and
aunts, or sisters and brothers of the faithful. The plots were
reserved for those less fortunate creatures, from whom the gates
of sanctified burial have been barred from antiquity. Canine and
feline, fish and fowl, rodent and reptile, and all manner of beast
were made welcome. The hallowed ground of Ashgrove was a
potter's field for pets.

April's cat, Fluffy, is buried there, as is Homer's hunting
dog, Fetch. Wanda's chinchilla named Chummy and Harriet's
Chihuahua, Peekaboo, have made the great journey over from
that ground. Flo's poodle, Bridgett, who practically lived and
worshiped at the church, rates a special memory garden. Many
goldfish and crayfish have fertilized the earth there, only to be
dug up in secret and transplanted to a vegetable patch nearby.
Hamsters and gerbils galore lie in its soil, and more little boys'
snakes than their mothers ever shook a stick at. Even Clyde
Parsens' old quarter horse, Quicksilver, was laid to rest on a
parcel of land nearby, though it took a backhoe and a dozen
shovels to finish the job.

This menagerie of a memorial park has been considered by
some a maudlin mockery of the dead. Such sentiment takes no
account of the ponderous power of pets to possess human
hearts. Many a family heirloom went down with a beast of the
field to rejoin nature in shared soil. Children's quilts, baby blankets, hand-crocheted mufflers, jewelry—all these and more have
been offered to the ground in gratitude for countless occasions
of pure, predictable pleasure. Such tokens answer to the universal tenets of experience: that pets are people as surely as are the
two-legged primates who claim them; that families are fashioned

as much from the sea of affection as from the pool of genes. Perhaps in an animal bone yard lies a vision not of the dead but the living—the promise of a blessed story yet to be told, God's grand finale of grace. It is a parable of harmony, high in the heavens and deep in the earth.

On an overcast August day, long after I had left Ashgrove Church, our family dog of thirteen years lay in Donna's lap, stealing her last loving breath. We wrapped Avignon in her favorite blanket and loaded her, several shovels, and our four young children into the family van. Then we headed out for a planting in hallowed ground. As we drove across town, the sky to the west began to clear, and a bit of late afternoon sun peeked out as light rain fell. At a moment bereft of cheer, a rainbow appeared. It painted the sky in a palette of gladness and then hung there like a colorful kite, just above our place of destination.

"Hey, look!" cried one child after another. "Mom! Dad! Look, up there! A rainbow! Avignon got a rainbow! Hey, Avignon," they shouted, "you got a rainbow!" In the shade of a myrtle, the rooty ground was broken with effort and dug to four feet. A flat stone and a fence-picket cross were placed to mark the grave. They remain there to this day. Our children's mementos of colored paper, ribbons, and macrame were the finishing touches. Then all four youngsters and two dog-tired adults joined hands and offered thanks to God for loss that stings in a love-revealing way. We bid farewell to the richer earth we'd made, but following behind us like a faithful pet was Avignon's rainbow, stubborn symbol of God's refusal to let the Lord's beloved go.

Someday I'll die and hope to be laid to rest in a patch of higher ground, under the shade of an oak or ash or elm. If the heavens shed a tear or two that day, it would be all right with me. Should it storm or sleet to mark my passing, I will name that an honor in advance. But a rainbow in the afternoon would be a cherished prize—a little one, like Avignon's, hanging in the western sky, unfurling its broad canopy of grace over hallowed ground.

FOUR

Sensitive Situations

. . . the teeth of everyone who eats sour grapes
shall be set on edge.
Jeremiah 31:30

You can get there from here,
but you have to pedal backwards.

14

The Bishop's Chair

Odd Anxious Seat

The Lord is in his holy temple,
the Lord's throne is in heaven:
his eyes behold, his eyelids try, the children of men.
Psalm 11:4 (KJV)

The sanctuary furnishings at Ashgrove Baptist Church were sparse and unspectacular. All were in mission-style oak or of an even later, still less elaborate period and motif. The grand exception was a great, dark walnut Gothic chair, standing out above the oak pews like Wilt Chamberlain at the jockey club. I took notice of the chair the first time I stepped inside the pastor's study. Its elaborate back resolved in a cornice, which met my gaze out the study window into the sanctuary. It shot up from the floor, dominating my view halfway to the top.

The story went that the chair had been rescued from a prestigious downtown church, scheduled for demolition. It had wound up on the chancel of the near eastside building, precursor to Ashgrove Church. No one could recollect who had brought it there, or by what means, or with what intent. When the congregation moved out to the county line, the "bishop's chair," as it was dubbed, came along. It was gingerly loaded onto a moving truck and whisked away to the new seat of worship, like the ark of the covenant, delivered to the city of David.

In the new sanctuary, the bishop's chair was first located just off the raised chancel, stage right of the American flag. After a number of years, it finally began to strike people as odd to have

such a massive chair, prominently placed, in which no one ever
sat. So it had been moved to the back of the church. There it
resided, in regal disuse, when I was called as pastor.

The chair made me anxious. Why *was* it there? What was its
purpose? Was it a Baptist reminder of what we are not, namely, a
people with any priestly center apart from the Word of God and
the believer's heart? Was it intended as temptation to a young
pastor with an Anglican streak just one shade away from showing?

The chair had a thick velvet seat cushion of scarlet. No doubt
many a distinguished man of the cloth had rested his rump there.
One of them along the way must have weighed in on the sumo-
wrestling side of the scales. The chair's concave contour left little
doubt that all underbracing had long since broken free. To sit
down there would have been to join the velvet underground, to
seep helplessly into its billowy plushness without a trace.

But my reticence over "the chair" went even deeper. Sitting
at my desk, whether in prayer, study, or reverie, I had the distinct
feeling of being watched. The corner of my eye caught the
silhouette of the chair back through the study window. From
peripheral sight and consciousness, I could conjure up countless
images for contemplation. The chair's trigabled cornice boasted
three ornamental crosses. These could have been the crosses on
Calvary. The trefoils in each gable resembled pairs of eyes, the
fancy scrollwork, little mouths. Or perhaps the three gables
represented the booths of the Transfiguration of Jesus, with
Moses and Elijah on either side. Or maybe they were Peter,
James, and John, the three disciples invited to witness the event.
The possibilities were endless—and tiresome. At some point I
had gone into the sanctuary and dragged the chair all the way to
the south wall out of view.

Even from the corner, the bishop's chair was a menacing
presence. As I preached, I began to envisage its hypothetical
occupants—former pastors and seminary professors, Luther,
Calvin, Jonathan Edwards, the angel Gabriel, Christ himself.
One after another, they sat sullenly in the bishop's chair, passing
judgment on my every word. This might actually have aided the
authenticity of my preaching. But it in no wise lessened the
strain of my delivery.

Worst of all was the congregation's largely unspoken expectation that, sooner or later, pastor and chair were destined to
come face to face—or bottom to seat, as it were. This came clear
through subtle hints and intimations, and especially through the

oral corpus of bishop's chair humor and folklore. There was the former pastor, Roy Shales, who had tripped over the chair during worship and bumped his head on a pew. He had been on one of his peripatetic tirades, prancing about with open Bible, when his right foot had caught the clawed base of the chair's left front leg. Roy had gone up, people said, and then Roy had come down, with such force that it appeared he had been hurled head over heels by an unknown power. One small child reported seeing an angel appear and extend a foot to accomplish the deed. But it disappeared again so quickly that she could not be certain. To whatever or whomever had been responsible, the congregation owed a debt of gratitude. Reverend Roy had gotten his comeuppance, and his come-downance. After conking his noggin, he had become a chastened Roy. And he had been much more apt at sermon time to keep to the safety of the pulpit. He only ventured out on special occasions, like Christmas and Communion Sunday, when the bishop's chair was removed to the south wall.

In another instance, an elderly deacon, while serving Communion, had backed up to the chair, lost his balance, and given it a decisive sitting down. The tray of fifty full Communion cups had splattered only slightly. But the deacon, who was rather stout, had sunk like an elephant in a bog. In his horror, he had taken pains to wriggle free. Instead, he managed only to turn the tray over in his lap. By then, other deacons had come to his aid, but in the heave and ho of the whole nasty business, Holy Communion splashed around like a burst water main. When the deacon finally escaped the chair's inscrutable grip, the volume of Welch's grape juice on the scene rivaled that of the blood Moses spattered on the Israelites at Sinai. It was not long after this frightful encounter that the unnamed deacon had gone on to the definitive debriefing of heaven. I couldn't help thinking of Uzzah who, in 2 Samuel, mistakenly touched the ark of the covenant in transit and paid the ultimate price. It was not a happy analogy, but it hung in the air, nonetheless, like the cloud of the Presence itself.

There were many such stories, most of which had the ring of authenticity. Since its removal to the back of the sanctuary, the bishop's chair had generated much less grist both for the fact and fable mills. Yet I sensed that, somehow, all this was soon to change. The chair was my anxious seat. It beckoned me come, but I resisted it.

The anxious seat, or mercy seat, also known as the "pen," was that place of contrition to which the spiritually anxious had fled in the camp meetings of the Revival in the West and in the Second Great Awakening. Such a seat or bench should be built sturdily, one might imagine, in order to withstand the manner of shaking and quaking, shivering and quivering. It required a thick coat of varnish to withstand the tears of remorse that fell in buckets, followed by the grateful tears of assurance and release, falling by the baptisteryful. Ashgrove Church had no anxious seat or mercy seat. Occasionally a worshiper might come forward in some manner of spiritual urgency and sit on the front pew. Mainline Baptists had all but abandoned the public display of contrition. The invitation itself was becoming a rarity. Conversions ought to be carried out with a restraint befitting serious and enlightened minds. I alone among moderns, it had seemed, still felt the tug of an anxious mourner toward a seat of uncertain judgment and mercy.

Much time passed. Pastor and "bishop" remained at a standoff. Then, as the spring of my first year arrived, the deacons came to me with a proposal. Chairman Herb Chestnut and his wife, Frances, had attended a reenactment of the Last Supper. Not since the passion play at the Scottish Rite Temple in Bloomington, Illinois, had they witnessed anything so stirring. It had been produced in a large church, a greatly elaborate affair. Why couldn't we hold a simpler version of such a service on Good Friday? The deacons proposed to set up a long table on the platform. It would be draped in purple and encircled by twelve folding chairs to accommodate the nine deacons and three volunteers. Each participant would represent a disciple, though no fancy speaking parts would be required.

"Mostly," Herb summed up, "we just need the Communion words and such, what Jesus said. . . ." Herb eyed me quizzically.

"Mind bein' Jesus?" he had finally managed.

"Jesus?" I responded in alarm.

"At the other church, the pastor was Jesus," Herb explained. "Why? Somethin' wrong with it?"

I told him I'd never thought about it. I would need a little time to consider the idea. I would get back with him that Sunday. However, as far as I was concerned, they were free to go ahead with their plans.

I, meanwhile, considered the invitation carefully. The whole question did seem to strike at the heart of my pastoral dilemma. Were I to play the role of Jesus, would I be making a mockery of

God or a mockery of myself? Or both? Or neither? Just how incarnational was my view of the pastorate? Was I God's representative at Ashgrove? Was I to manifest something uniquely spiritual that the congregation not merely desired, but required? Or should a pastorate point so far away from itself it might be mistaken for an off-ramp exit sign on an interstate highway? Biblical counsel appeared vague. In 2 Corinthians, Paul spoke of boasting about our weaknesses, that Christ's power might be in us. Which, then, should be visible to the world, the power or the weakness? Wasn't the risk of idolatry in personality-based pastorates almost a justification for at least a mild ineptitude? Had not the emphasis on personal charisma led congregants too often into the belief that a particular pastoral style, or technique, or race, or gender was the indispensable sign of God's presence? I retreated to my study to reason it out. The whole while I could sense the bishop's chair, peering in at me from window's edge, curious as to where I'd finally take my seat on the subject.

The following Sunday morning, Herb arrived at the church prepared to announce the Last Supper idea to the congregation. It was going to be an exciting event, Herb had pitched. Deacons would be in costume. Lights would be dimmed. All the old hymns would be sung. The Lord's Supper would be served.

"The preacher *might* even play Jesus!" Herb had added in an ironic tone that seemed rehearsed. "But, we'll be needin' three volunteers to be the other disciples. If any of you here are interested, please let me know! Thank you."

Herb had meant, of course, to say we needed other "men" to play disciples. But, instead, he had said "volunteers." Heidi Hapness had heard him clearly and, as always, literally. She was a deaconess, serving her first term in that official capacity, serving her first term in *any* official capacity, in fact. Heidi was guileless and sweet as cherry pie filling, but "her elevator don't go all the way to the top," as Bert put it.

"Well *I'll* be one!" Heidi had exclaimed, right there, in the middle of Herb's speech, in the middle of worship. Herb pretended not to hear. But Heidi was already turning around to confer with Anna Quarfarth, who was also a deaconess. "Me 'n' Anna here, we can do that! Right, Anna?"

Anna looked pained. She smiled one of her tight smiles, and that was all.

Herb sat down quickly, and worship continued. But immediately following the benediction, Heidi was all over him, like flies on potato salad. Which disciple could she be? What about

the one who was like a rock? Or maybe the one that wrote John
3:16? But it didn't really matter, because they were all Jesus'
disciples. We're all Jesus' disciples, too, right? And on and on
she babbled like water in a brook, and just as wearing.

Herb looked helplessly in my direction, but I only shrugged
and smiled.

"Choose deaconesses," I told him later. "Get three deaconesses, and I'll play Jesus. At this point, you're stuck with Heidi
anyway." Herb had not been pleased. Women had never served
Communion at Ashgrove Church before, he had said.

"I've never been Jesus Christ before," I retorted.

"What will Gibson say?" Herb had wondered. Gibson was
vice chairman of the board and resident standard-bearer for the
fundamentalist cause. Herb would have to talk it over with the
other deacons. He would be in touch.

The following week, we were all gathered together for a
read through. Only Gibson had rejected the idea of women
disciples. He had stormed out of the deacons meeting, vowing
never to return. No one minded particularly, since he did this
with the frequency some smokers give up cigarettes.

"It's a special occasion, men!" Herb had argued. "I can't
see it could do no harm."

Heidi, Addie Cox, who chaired the deaconess board, and
Gladys Hatch, who wasn't then a deaconess but had been in the
past, agreed to serve. They were to be cast in the roles of
Thomas, Jude Thaddeus, and Simon the Zealot.

"Who's Thomas again?" Heidi asked.

"The one who touched Jesus' hands and side," I answered.

"Wow!" she said.

No one had been willing to take the role of Judas. The deacons had already divided up the "good roles," and none even
entertained the thought of swapping his away. In the "upper
room" at Ashgrove, at least, Judas would be invited and encouraged to bug out early.

The Communion service was to conclude our Good Friday
worship. On cue, deacons and deaconesses would process to
their places at the table, as the lights were dimmed. I had prepared a disciples' digest of one-paragraph speeches for them to
recite. I would quote from Jesus' farewell discourse and conclude with the institution of the Supper. The disciples were
responsible for their own "authentic" attire.

On Good Friday evening, I was running late. At 6:50 P.M. before the 7:00 service, I ran from the car with a white bathrobe in tow and headed straight to the men's room to change. By the time I strolled into the sanctuary and made my way to the chancel, the pianist and song leader were commencing with a string of rousing hymns. The third selection was "Face to Face," and it was on the chorus that I finally came face-to-face with the awful truth. In a fashion I took at the time to be as wily as Satan himself, the deacons had removed the metal folding chair at the table's midpoint. In its place, towering ominously to the very height of the raised baptistery, was the bishop's chair. Here, on Black Friday, wood of consequence had finally overtaken God's humble servant.

At the appointed hour, the disciples came forward and stood in their places. In turn, they spoke their pieces and were seated at the table. I, meanwhile, had slipped in between table and bishop's chair in the manner of a beekeeper who forgot his protective outerwear. The chair jutted out so far from the rail that I had to bend my knees just to stand there. With the roll call of the "eleven" completed, it was my turn. I began by reading from John, chapter 17, Jesus' extended prayer to the Father, in which he makes clear that both his strength and weakness are offered in unambiguous service to the glory of God. "[G]lorify your Son so that the Son may glorify you. . . ." And further, that we, the people of God, share in that glory, "so that the world may know that you . . . have loved them, even as you have loved me." It is to *God's* glory that we are what we are, and do what we do, and stand, and fall, and endeavor to accomplish the works of love for yet another day.

I concluded with Christ's invitation to the Supper, as I broke bread and served the men and women, who departed together out among the congregation and did likewise. And then at long last, after ten months of evasion and delay, I surrendered my ministerial fortunes to the care of God, and I sat down.

"Yeh looked awful small up there in that big chair, Preacher," commented Alberta Rump afterward, out in the vestibule. "But yeh got out of it okay, and that part kindy surprised us! Everybody done a real nice job. Lotsa us got teary-eyed tonight!"

"Thanks, Bert," I said.

Gibson and his wife, Betty, had not attended. Everyone present, however, had received the bread and cup with a glad heart, from the hands of the disciples of Jesus—male and female. Each one had offered the presence of Christ to all who came seeking God's favor and grace. After all, that was the purpose of ministry.

The bishop's chair was returned to its place in the back corner. Occasionally, I would retire to it for some lofty thinking and grand dreaming. As far as I know, that is where it has remained, right up to the present time and the current pastor— if, that is, she knows what's good for her!

15

Weddings

Bad Omens

. . . there shall once more be heard
the voice of mirth and the voice of gladness,
the voice of the bridegroom and the voice of the bride,
the voices of those who sing, as they bring thank offerings to the house
    of the Lord:
"Give thanks to the Lord of hosts, for the Lord is good,
for his steadfast love endures forever!"
                                                    Jeremiah 33:10–11

Like most other things in my maiden pastorate, the first "walk down the aisle" caught me flat-footed. Hassie Longstreet's grand-niece, Farrah, arrived from Baton Rouge, ostensibly to be near her mother, Heather, Hassie's niece. Heather had divorced Farrah's father five years earlier and relocated to the far west side of Indianapolis under somewhat secretive circumstances. Hassie had followed her heart and niece north. Drawn to proper nouns, like *Baptist,* but not prone to bother with modifiers, like *northern* or *southern, liberal,* or *conservative,* Hassie had quickly discovered our quaint little church in the grove and made it her new home. The good people of Ashgrove had greeted the southerner with open arms. They had eagerly banked on her sizable tithe as well.

Farrah and her sister, Faye, had chosen to remain with their father and the life they knew in Louisiana. Then, at eighteen, Farrah had ventured out on her own, or so early appearances suggested. Arriving at Indianapolis, she had moved in with Mom "just until I get on my feet," as she put it. Within two weeks of her appearance, a male friend had come to call, all the way from down home in Creole country. Jayce Omer was pushing forty and happily unemployed. He had immediately opened a bank account. He claimed to have come into a large inheritance, but Heather Longstreet was no stranger to the prevarications of strange men. She had rummaged around for the truth, and when this came to nought, she had gone right to the source and throttled it out of him. Jayce Omer had won a seemingly spurious physical injury suit and was sitting pretty on some unknown sum. After several days it had become clear that it was disappearing like water down a rain sewer—exactly like it, as far as Heather was concerned. Jayce had been living it up in a local three-star hotel, Jacuzzi and wet bar included, and Farrah had been staying out so late "of an evenin'," Hassie reported, that it was practically "of a mornin'" when she had been coming in.

Just as Heather had determined to wage war for the good of her little girl, Farrah and Jayce dropped a bombshell. They had come home after dark and surprised Heather in her nightgown. Farrah appeared giddy with delight as Jayce, in that whimsical way of his that Heather despised, had said, "Hey, sweetpea!— Think yo mama deah betta' sit down fo' this one!"

And so she had, which turned out to have been a very good idea. They were to be wed, Farrah announced—immediately!

The stages of grief had ensued, but Heather and Hassie's strong southern spirits had emerged intact. Past the shock and the grief, the anger and the bargaining, there had come the chastened realization that, short of murder or castration, nuptials were assured. Thoughtfully, they had turned their energies to the question of the solemn ceremony—which is how they regarded it. Should this union be in the sight of God, or should they spare the Almighty one more worldly embarrassment? There was always the chance that, if *God* sealed the bond, it might actually "take," a risk they could scarcely stomach. But if they counseled Farrah against a church ceremony, would they not be endangering her immortal soul? And what made them think she would heed the advice of a divorcee and an old maid, anyway? In the end, they placed their bets on a merciful God and their faith in the services of the Lord's humble representative at Ashgrove Church.

Ministers hate weddings. Not all will admit this openly, but among cloistered clergy there is little disagreement. While there are exceptions to every rule, I am suspicious of the pastor who doesn't chafe at the thought of another Saturday afternoon stolen away from the family, a favorite fishing hole, or even playing backyard bond servant to one's own honeybunch. More to the point is the widespread lack of interest in the venerable mysteries of marriage. Once a holy tryst, an act of profound theological moment, modern marriage is at best a contract and at worst a long-odds gamble. And, notwithstanding a serious stab at premarital counseling, the minister cannot escape the impression that the quixotic couple is not listening.

Seasoned preachers are under no illusion that congregants follow the stream of any sermon from beginning to end. Clergy have every reason to loathe the routine business of the church, with its endless parade of incompatible opinion. And they discover early on in every form of counseling that, unlike a carpenter or plumber, they cannot "fix" people. But at least most parishioners arrive on the Sabbath with the good intentions to hear the Word rightly divided, and at least the church's business is family business in which the pastor is an equal partner, and at least those with needs have come freely to seek advice, not only barely to stomach it.

With weddings, by contrast, the sanctuary is a space to rent and the preacher is a hired hand, a line item on the wedding package, right above the aisle runner, sound booth, and birdseed. While enormously cynical about the preacher's place in the American institution of marriage, I have resisted the temptation to shun it altogether. I remember that, save for the graces of the most important pastors of my life, including my uncle, best friend, and pastor of my youth, my wife and I would not have tied the nuptial knot. And now and then, there are still mainline couples who thoughtfully opt for a church wedding, though generally, as in the case of Jayce and Farrah, either bride or groom is some congregant's next-of-kin.

I was watching the clock with one aggravated eye, and the gravel drive with the other. Anger has that way of making one see double. It was 6:25 P.M. before a 7:15 rendezvous with my wife at an area restaurant. We ate dinner out only seldom, and it was good for our marriage when we did. It paid an even sweeter dividend when I managed to be within ten minutes or so of punctual. Now, a capricious pair whose holy matrimony was in jeopardy before it began was compounding the strife of another member of that endangered species, "clergy couple."

I had been measuring Farrah and Jayce's tardiness as well by the number of jet airplanes that had raced overhead since straight up seven o'clock. I had worried that the airport's proximity to the church would addle my brains as greatly as the pastorate itself. But over the weeks since my arrival, I had ceased except in rare moments of idleness even to note the moan of turbos and landing gear. Many parishioners attested to this adaptation. Harold Hatch even claimed to have no recollection of the first jet screaming immediately above him as he painted the famed Ashgrove steeple.

At this point in my pastorate, I was just beginning to under-stand. But on this occasion, the deafening screech of jet turbos, marking the early evening spate of airline arrivals, was boring into me like a dentist's drill.

The count was two Boeings, three McDonnell Douglasses, and a high-flying Hornet, heading north to a nearby air base, when, racing into the drive at similar decibel levels, came Jayce's blazing black Trans Am. The pair shuffled to the door with scarcely a word, and I showed them into my study. They sat facing me in straight-back chairs set side by side and fidgeted with each other's fingers like squirrels in a friendly squabble. At the same time, they had set their faces in a posture of ironic defiance. While Farrah had twice attended worship with her Great-Aunt Hassie—Heather only came on the odd Sunday—we had established no rapport, and she seemed to have prepared herself for the worst of clerical interrogations. Jayce, fifteen years my senior, appeared hell-bent on remaining aloof, treating me like a little brother conducting a family interview for a class assignment.

Indeed, I did ask a slough of questions: when and how did they first meet, what did they share in common, what of their families of origin, of what significance was their age difference, what would be their plans as a couple. Jayce, I was not surprised to learn, had been married twice before. He had no children, at least that he knew about. He had made a lot of mistakes but had learned his lesson, he said. And now he had his little flower, Farrah—a new reason to live and to "do right." As for the age difference, Farrah was every bit as mature as he, Jayce assured me. I had little doubt of it. Still, the pretension meter was screaming. It brought to mind a politician who justifies a policy flip-flop reflecting new voter preferences. Farrah, meanwhile, was lapping up his every word like a puppy dog.

Eventually, I worked my way into a decidedly more esoteric, theological line of inquiry: why did they desire a church wed-ding, why the services of a Baptist pastor, why get married at all, what did marriage mean in the modern world, what did God and the gospel of Jesus Christ have to do with the marriage covenant, and so on. These questions went by and large unanswered. I managed to keep things alive only by engaging in what in legal parlance is called "leading the witness." Farrah had from time to time attended church in Baton Rouge with her family and later with her fraternal grandmother, but her practical Christian experience was scant. Jayce was a Roman Catholic who had shunned organized religion, deeming it pretentious and proving once again how profoundly we can be shaped by that which we reject.

The session fizzled, and reluctantly we all agreed to meet again the following week. At that time we would make some decisions. I invited the aspiring couple to Sunday worship and closed with a prayer for God's guidance in relationships, mine no less than theirs. It was 7:30 P.M. as I sped away to save a marriage over fettucine Alfredo and spumoni ice cream. Pushing the speed limit, I could not help but wonder whether Farrah, Jayce, and I might not ourselves be about to race off a cliff.

In the morning, having slept on the matter, not to mention on the couch, I made a decision, despite serious misgivings, to proceed with Farrah's wedding. It was not that I had any confidence she and Jayce would succeed as a couple. Statistically, a majority of marital relationships I would seal before God would end bitterly in divorce. But Jayce and Farrah were determined to be wed, one way or the other. Given the opportunity to intertwine their hopes and the gospel's, it seemed incumbent upon me at least to attempt to do so.

After two additional sessions, I had covered the prenuptial bases and planned with them a somewhat simple ceremony for a Saturday wedding in September. Heather and Hassie had been pleased. My closing pitch to them had been that marriage was a mine field. It would require faith and fortitude. And God would need to be in the midst of them if they hoped even to have a chance.

The rehearsal had been scheduled for the morning of the wedding. Farrah's father and sister had flown in on a red-eye the night before. While things proceeded somewhat smoothly, at the conclusion of the run-through I was bombarded by a whole host of questions I had no idea how to address—matters to which I had given no more heed than the proper temperature for serving tea: when should the ushers seat the mothers; and where and in what order, when should the candles be lighted; what if a ring

dropped and rolled under a pew; what if Farrah couldn't repeat
her vows; where should the receiving line begin and who should
be in it; was I supposed to fill out the marriage license or were
they; and so on.

Here was my day of reckoning for having spurned practical
ministry courses in order to double up on speculative theology
and philosophy. That afternoon my only speculation was as to
whether I would close the day without becoming a laughing-
stock. Fifteen minutes before the wedding hour, I was phoning
the seminary professor who taught the course I had neglected to
take. The professor was unavailable. I was all too happy to settle
for his wife. Clearly, no one on earth knew less at that moment
about wedding protocol than I. I pumped her with questions
and took her answers as the sweet gospel truth. Then I washed
my trembling hands free of sweat and other potential vicissi-
tudes, said a prayer to the same effect, and joined the business
of marital union, American style.

The wedding had proceeded remarkably smoothly, with
only one minor mishap. Farrah had, indeed, dropped Jayce's
ring. It hit the carpet and began to roll like a stone away from
both of them. The devil himself couldn't have concocted a more
ominous sign of things to come, I had thought. Yet suddenly it
had whirled right under Ed Garrett's shiny left shoe. He was
standing up for Jayce at Hassie's request. They had formed an
instant affinity—perhaps the attraction of new money to old, or
old money to new, or, more likely, just of money to itself. Characteristically, Ed had swooped the ring up like a runaway silver
dollar and had it back in Farrah's hands PDQ.

After a week's honeymoon in destinations unknown, Jayce
and Farrah were back in town and settling in. This surprised us
all, and none more than Heather and Hassie. To no one's surprise, however, they had avoided church like the winter flu. We
saw them only once that fall, on the first Sunday after Thanksgiving.
They had arrived with Hassie, wearing matching red and green
Christmas tree sweatshirts, but then they had melted away again
like a wet snow.

On two occasions I tracked down Farrah and Jayce at their
apartment, ten miles north and east into the city. On my first
visit, the house was littered with records, tapes, games, and
gadgets of every description. Every day was a good day for a
shopping spree, I gathered. The Trans Am, which turned out to
be a rental, had been turned back in. Farrah and Jayce had taken

to riding the bus but never came home empty-handed. The only furniture in the big apartment was a dining set, a large sectional couch, and a waterbed. Clothes were stacked or strewn across the floor in every room. During my second visit, a repo man came for the stereo. It went peacefully, without a fight. Only because of my presence, I think, had Jayce contained himself. To Jayce, it must have been just one more stroke of the pen against organized religion.

This was the last time I saw Jayce. Clearly the credit pipeline was running dry. A four-month, nonstop carnival ride was screeching to a halt. He and Farrah had begun to fight nearly incessantly. Between each skirmish he would disappear. Hours later he would return all shnockered up, and the battle of words would continue. As far as I could tell, he never struck Farrah. "Mah mama raised a geeentleman!" he once had declared. But there was not the first hint of gentleness left between them.

On a frigid day in early January, Jayce left at night, having scraped and pawned his way to the price of a one-way bus fare to Baton Rouge. Indiana winters were too chilly for his taste, he had concluded. Marriage was, too. After thirty-six hours, Farrah had come to grips with the obvious—Jayce wasn't coming back. By then, she had been waitressing for several weeks at a pancake house. She threw down her apron, emptied out the apartment, and moved back in with her mother.

The next Sunday, Farrah was sitting nervously in church. She was flanked by Hassie and Heather, who had come to offer joyous thanksgiving to God. It was not immediately clear why Farrah was there, but it seemed a positive step. For most of the service her head remained bowed. I imagined prayers of penance and regret, but more likely she was concealing mascara runs. Either way, the sabbath celebration was attaining one of its chief aims: to bathe weary pilgrims in the grace and majesty of God.

Then had come the closing hymn, "Just As I Am," one of our hymns of periodic plunge into full crusade fervor. But the moment was soul stirring. Farrah had stood suddenly between the two persons in the world who loved her best, and they had placed arms around her trembling waist. What Heather wanted, and Hassie with her, is what every mother desires for her daughter: her daughter's happiness, and, if that proves elusive, then at least the absence of anguish and pain. At the moment neither condition held, but Farrah was reaching out again, "just as she was," and a spinster and divorcée were stretching back to meet her, and the Lamb of God was in the midst of them.

For a matter of months Farrah remained with her mother, just one more pair for the swelling ex files of American marriage. Eventually, she returned to the land of the Bayou, where she married a Southern Baptist from Shreveport. I know nothing of the circumstances of that union, but I imagine the officiating minister gave up a good Saturday afternoon gator hunt to perform the ceremony. I am also certain that he knew exactly where and when to seat a proud mother and how to keep wedding rings from rolling across state lines. I have it on grateful authority that the rings have remained firmly on fingers for already many years and counting.

16

Gibson

Tale of Self-inflicted Bondage

. . . passing judgment on another you condemn yourself. . . .
Romans 2:1

Divorce was the issue. Divorce, and one little verse from the Gospel according to Matthew. I had thought often that these words, like many in Scripture, might serve as either windows to heaven or to a hell on earth. In 1979, Gibson Mayes had married his wife, Betty—three years after his first wife's death to cancer, three years after Betty had emerged from a bitter divorce. By many measures, theirs was a tender and loving relationship. Still, on the day of their marriage, Gibson had wedded some deep biblical trouble.

Gibson was a self-styled Christian fundamentalist, a seasoned despiser of all loose strands in the knot of biblical interpretation. The text said the meaning and meant the saying. The text said that men who married divorcées were adulterers. The words proceeded from the lips of Jesus.

Betty had strong ties to the Ashgrove congregation, having schooled with several of the church's women, including Addie Cox and Anna Quarfarth. Betty had always viewed participation in a church as a relational bond, a precious, human interchange rounding out a private life. Like many of the Ashgrove faithful, she had little interest in doctrinal subtleties or biblical certitudes. She wanted to come to church looking her best and to leave church feeling her best.

Gibson, meanwhile, had joined the Ashgrove family and quickly created for himself a new position in the church: guardian of orthodoxy. Gibson sparred with supposed heresy like a back-alley boxer. He picked fights sometimes even before he knew who the opponent was. After I had crossed gloves with Gibson once or twice, Harold Hatch had motioned me to a corner and filled me in on Gibson's fighting career.

Once, during the pastorate of Milton Hawkes, Gibson had left Ashgrove Church in protest. The issue had been the authorship of the first five books of the Old Testament, the Pentateuch. Gibson was sure they were penned by Moses. Following conservative scholars, he argued that either Moses wrote it *all,* or it was a "patchwork fabrication of men." Milton, always the concerned teacher, had launched a mild rebuttal, advocating a richness of God-inspired traditions, woven into the Law of Moses over much time.

"*Jesus* said Moses wrote it!" Gibson had roared.

"Jesus said Moses *wrote,*" Milton responded, "but not that he wrote the *whole first five books of the Bible!* And how did Moses write about his own death at the very end of it?" Milton had wanted to know.

"Well, if Jesus could rise from the dead, then Moses could write about his own death!" Gibson had responded.

This exchange had gone on for the last half hour of a Wednesday evening Bible study. It had continued out on the lawn until the mosquitoes Moses said God created had eaten the two men alive. Finally, Gibson had stormed off, dragging behind him a reluctant Betty, looking her best and feeling her worst. He had found temporary contentment at an independent, fundamental church down the road. There, pastor and people took the unqualified truth as seriously as Gibson did. In that church, he had surmised, he would be able to serve unreservedly. He might become a deacon and help safeguard true belief.

But Jesus had spoken plainly in Matthew, chapter 5, that anyone who marries a divorced woman commits adultery. The apostle Paul had told Timothy unequivocally that deacons should be married only once. This new, unimpeachable brotherhood had been all too happy to welcome Gibson to the pews. They had eagerly accepted his tithe. But as to his assumption of leadership within their church, Gibson had to be kidding!

So in due course, Gibson had returned to Ashgrove, an embarrassed Betty behind him. He was serving as deacon and chief defender of dogma when I arrived on the scene. Soon he was preying on my every word—taking jabs, mixing punches, searching out a new opponent's hidden weakness. Sooner or later we both knew that things between us were headed for verbal fisticuffs.

At last Gibson discovered the opening he had sought. During my first year as pastor, I conducted a Bible study on Paul's letter to the Romans. By the time I reached chapter 2, Gibson had jumped back into the ring, and this time the gloves came off. The crux of the question was grace. How radical was it? Did the scales of scriptural truth tilt in its direction? Or did the weight of human iniquity tip the balance toward the law and divine retribution? This was the problem with "you liberals," Gibson contended. They misjudged the radical nature of *sin*. This was the problem with "ultra-conservatives," I countered. They misjudged the radical nature of *grace*.

Specifically, I had followed in Romans a line of interpretation that identified Paul's long list of sins, concluding chapter 1, as instances of a universal iniquity. Sin is as sweeping as God's gracious broom of redemption. We are all caught up in its curse. Therefore, however heinous might appear to us the trespasses of others, they pale next to the arrogant self-righteousness of self-appointed judges. "For God shows no partiality," and "you have no excuse, whoever you are, when you judge others. . . ." Thus, it was misguided to single out anything or anyone from Paul's list for special condemnation. Such a practice, I argued, was at odds with our own reception of grace. Yet, strangely, I thought, this kind of thing occurred constantly in the church.

I wanted badly to ask Gibson if he himself didn't know what this was like—if he hadn't experienced personally the sting of such prejudicial thinking. But I restrained myself. Instead, all that Gibson concluded from my words was that I was "soft on sin." If I continued to teach such things, he said, I inevitably would sanction all kinds of wickedness. It is "the doers of the law," he quoted Paul, "who shall be justified." With that, Gibson seemed to have cast lots with the countless souls who elect to live life on the fringes of grace. He left Ashgrove Church again, a bedraggled Betty behind him, both looking and feeling her worst. Returning to the independent brethren down the road, they resembled a pair of migratory birds, coming and going by season. And though Gibson was again a bird caged in the pews, there at least the flock could carry his tune. Lovers of taut ropes walk through life on very short leashes.

17

Funerals

Final Words

Do not hide your face from me,
or I shall be like those who go down to the Pit.
Let me hear of your steadfast love in the morning,
for in you I put my trust.
Teach me the way I should go,
for to you I lift up my soul.
Psalm 143:7–8

Folks die—people of faith right along with everyone else. The Ashgrove congregation and its pastor were fortunate in that most all the men of the church were robust and the women ageless. Even so, from time to time Azrael would stop around to take a soul or two home to heaven. Death makes no distinctions. In all times and places, it casts anchor often enough to keep alive the great question of death's meaning—for the dead as well as the living.

The first funeral of my pastoral ministry was of an elderly woman and long-standing member of Ashgrove Church. To this day I count it my good fortune to have been initiated into the rite of the dead through a life such as hers. Rosy was well-loved by all. She died as all would wish—in her own bed with her family gathered around her. I, too, was invited to her side. It was requested that I pray the Lord's Prayer, and without hesitation I began, "The Lord is my Shepherd, I shall not want . . . ," and I forged ahead, all the way down to "the house of the LORD," before catching my mistake. No one seemed perturbed. Rosy had already slipped quietly into a coma. Over the space of an hour the labor of breathing gently subsided. Color left her face and extremities. A visiting nurse took her pulse. After a few minutes, she took it again and then once more. Satisfied, she brushed the palm of her hand tenderly over Rosy's eyelids until they were firmly closed for the last time. Then she pulled the sheet up around Rosy's shoulders, leaving a single arm exposed. While she contacted the funeral home, family members gave Rosy a last embrace. They squeezed her hand. Quietly, they consoled each other and wiped away one another's tears. Then, one by one, they filed from the room. Regardfully, Rosy's eldest daughter closed the door to just a crack, as does a mother whose restless child has finally dozed into peaceful sleep.

Never before had I been encamped so near the scene of death or witnessed that gray twilight in which life and death grow indistinguishable. I had seen relatives in the coffin. As a small child, I had peered over the box into my grandmother's lifeless face. But I was told and had accepted that this earthly shell was not really she. Grandmother belonged to God, and God belonged in the realm of heaven, and that is where she had gone to stay as well. Up close, the advent of death seemed far from the frightening specter in the popular mind. Rosy had lived a life of ninety-two years with few if any regrets. I learned that day that death possesses a great poignancy. At its highest, it is an occasion bathed in dignity and grace. Rosy's memorial service was a celebration of a charmed life, confidently commended into the eternal care of a loving Lord.

The sublimity of death is rarely so clear-cut. My second funeral was that of a milliner, a seller of hats, from back in the days when one might still specialize in a particular garment accessory, whether hats or scarves, neckties or hosiery. My services had been requested by her daughter, Sally, a member of our church who had come to the faith following marriage to Winslow Cox's son, Philip. Her milliner mother, Victoria, had not merely sold hats. She had worn hats, and she had slept in them. She had preached hats and practically worshiped them. Hats were her life. In the seventies, Victoria had become aware of the deleterious effects of the sun on human skin. This had added appreciably to her zeal for hats. They were more than mere statements of style and fashion. Hats saved lives. If you wore a hat religiously every trip out-of-doors, then, while you might still die in a car accident, develop liver disease from

alcohol consumption or lung cancer from smoking, you at least
would be safe from skin cancer. And your skin would maintain its
natural beauty long after your friends became shriveled speci-
mens of tanned cowhide.

In her sixty-first year, Victoria had been diagnosed with
melanoma. After numerous surgeries on her face and torso
which left her silken skin in tatters, doctors had informed her
that the cancer had metastasized to her major organs. Within
three months, she was gone. Her many clients arrived at the
mortuary in bonnets, pillboxes, coifs, and derbies. Victoria herself was laid to rest in her favorite Louise Bourbon.

Clearly, death was fickle, subject not only to the whims of
the sun's rays but profoundly influenced by that lottery of nature
known as the gene pool. At Victoria's funeral, my homily was at
best an awkward attempt to relate the life of one who loved a
"good look" to the loveliness of a Savior, and the blessed shelter
of a good hat to God's promise of perpetual protection. I spoke
of the whole armor of God by which we withstand the day of evil,
and I did not give short shrift to the mighty helmet of salvation—
a touch that Victoria would have deemed apropos, if not very
fashionable. But deeper questions lingered in the air: Was death
itself evil? Was all loss, all robbery of life, intrinsically wicked? Or
could anything so inevitable, so basic to life as death, be aptly
described in such perverse terms? Wasn't death just death,
merely a mark of our finitude, the natural price of having been
born? If death and the suffering in its wake were evil, then what
role did a benevolent God play in it? Many pinned on Scripture
the equating of death's curse with human sin. But where did this
leave an unlucky milliner? Where did it leave a baby blown away
in a hurricane, or a trailer park family twisted apart in a tornado,
or annual monsoon victims in Bangladesh, or drought victims in
Somalia?

These were among the questions I brought to my next rendezvous with death. I was contacted by a local hospital in search
of a minister. A mother of two, still in her twenties, was in the
advanced stages of leukemia. She would most certainly die
within days or weeks. The family had declared no church affiliation but had requested a visit from someone of the Baptist
persuasion.

On the hospital's oncology floor, her room had that distinctive malodor of cellular civil war, of one's flesh waging a battle
against itself. The woman's name was Cynthia, and to behold her

was to be in a single instant both drawn and repulsed. She was the image of beauty caught fast in the grip of unseemliness. Her eyes were sunken amid circles of darkened skin, and they drew you down like deep portholes into a tale of long torment. A morphine drip managed her pain, holding her mere milliliters above the waterline of agony, yet leaving her barely lucid. Still, as she gathered herself in my presence, I sensed in her a core of strength that I could connect only with her love of her life, her family, her children. I introduced myself and groped for words of comfort. As I knelt at her bed and prayed, she hovered between wakefulness and sleep. I, too, was drawn into a hypnotic silence, as if Christ himself had commandeered the moment to pronounce a blessing upon my own feebleness no less than Cynthia's.

The silence was broken abruptly by Cynthia's mother, Hilda, who had returned from the cafeteria. She had spent another dutiful night at the hospital so Cynthia's husband could attend to their daughter and son. Hilda must likewise have been fatigued. She undoubtedly knew at that moment her own deep sorrow and fear. Yet Hilda was one of that group of souls who turn the denial of raw feeling into their lifework. Within two minutes of conversation she had first proposed and then confirmed her theory of God's plan at work in her daughter's suffering. God of course was all powerful, she began. Everything that happened was within the scope of God's intention. God *knew* all things as well—past, present and future. In perfect omniscience, God had glimpsed some looming catastrophe in her daughter's life. In an act of supreme mercy, God had stricken Cynthia with leukemia, had visited upon her its immense suffering unto death, had caused her to be ripped away from her husband and small children and any earthly future, all in order to spare her that untold tragedy, compared to which her current anguish was but a bothersome hangnail.

Through her lengthy pontification, I kept glancing at Cynthia, assuring myself that she was indeed safely asleep—not that I hadn't read that our minds hear and often recall things uttered as we dream. Given Hilda's brashness, it seemed improbable at any rate that Cynthia had been spared her mother's theories about her illness up to this point. More likely, they greeted her each morning, guided her every waking hour, and tucked her in at night. Meanwhile, I was thinking fast to formulate some response, to offer some counter to Hilda's faith, indeed to Hilda's God.

God did not cause cancer, I endeavored to assure her. Cancer was a risk of a world of radically free will—not only among human beings, but atoms and molecules and cellular mutations such as precipitated Cynthia's leukemia. Yes, God did create that world, and so God was ultimately responsible for all things within it. But the power God exercised amid such unbridled freedom, whether out of choice or necessity, did not cause harm such as her daughter suffered. Rather, God was at work redeeming real evil and suffering through the gift of enduring love, ceaselessly and persuasively offered. This was the message of the cross of Christ, I reminded her. And this was why I could still kneel at her daughter's bedside and pray in hope to the God both of creation and salvation. I didn't like the evil of cancer any more than she, I told Hilda. But turning it into a good, though inexplicable, act of God would not make the evil go away. It would still manage to hurt and confound us. It could bring us to our knees. Evil would continue to be evil. But evil could only destroy us by causing us to deny the goodness of God.

Hilda's eyes had a glazed-over look as I spoke, as if she had raised an invisible shield to bar all unsolicited thoughts. Seasoned in the art of evasion, she quickly turned the subject elsewhere. I promised to come again and asked her to call the church were there any change in her daughter's status. Then I took leave of that room of dim prospects and even darker reasoning.

Two days later the call came. Cynthia had fallen into a coma. She had died shortly thereafter. Her husband Randy asked me to conduct the memorial service, and I agreed. He and I had met only briefly in a hospital corridor. But a door had opened between us almost immediately, as often happens in crisis. Pain seeks solace where it can, and bewilderment holds vigil for the dawning of clarity. There had been scarcely any time for what little I had to offer of either. Still, he had called on me, and for that I was gratified.

The funeral was to be held at a mortuary on the far south side of town. I arrived there to greet the family on the afternoon before the service, just prior to the public viewing. I stood at the casket with Randy, and we beheld Cynthia's peaceful countenance. Gone were the signs of struggle and the lines of pain. All had been carefully concealed beneath greasepaint, powder, and rouge. Meanwhile, Randy was straining to surface that shipwreck of emotions so common at such times—deep sadness, tempered by an overwhelming sense of relief, kindling in turn feelings of guilt. Buried beneath it all was anger turned white-hot bitter. Combined, it was pathos of unknown ballast.

Randy was in a cathartic moment when Hilda arrived. She put a smothering arm on Randy's shoulder and doused his passion with platitudes. Well, she started in, wasn't it lovely—the Lord had taken their Cynthia home with him! We knew of course it had all been to save her from something truly horrible. We didn't know what quite, but now she was with the Lord. Now dear Cynthia was safe and sound. . . . And on Hilda went, cataloguing God's arsenal of means to bend all events to the divine unalterable will. This need to safeguard God's supreme sovereignty over every infinitesimal occurrence of life seemed to be woven into Hilda's every fiber. Whether planted by some early influence or arising from her own inner voice, it must have taken hold at roughly the age she learned to lace her own shoes. By now, it was firmly tied down with a tight double knot—much as Hilda herself. My remarks at the hospital had not even penetrated Hilda's ear wax. As far as she was aware, we had never before spoken on the subject. This time I smiled and nodded and said nothing. No uttered word would have made the slightest difference.

At Cynthia's memorial service, I took as text Paul's word of supreme comfort in Romans, chapter 8. Paul did not set out there to deny the reality of peril, hardship, or distress. Nor did Paul pin human suffering on the will of God. Evil and suffering were among the givens of the present age. In anguish, the whole creation groaned inwardly. But it was in the midst of bona fide evil that true goodness was made known, and that goodness was God's nature and God's redemption in Christ Jesus. Because God *was* good, God was at work in all things *for* good. Situations might not resolve when and how we would like. Not everything was yet ready to cooperate with God's loving intentions for the world. But through the witness of the cross and resurrection, it was pretty clear the direction in which God was aiming.

Meanwhile, there was nothing good about Cynthia's death. It was a tragic reality, the world was poorer for her loss, and God did not approve. But God loved Cynthia. Nothing in all creation could separate her from that love, in Christ Jesus. And it was through loving God and one another that *we* participated in

God's work of redemption. Such love was the greatest act of faith available to us in the midst of human adversity, and the finest way to honor Cynthia and her brave struggle.

At the close of the service, I stood by the casket as friends filed past in somber procession. Next came the immediate family—Cynthia's sister, an aunt and uncle, Randy's mother and father, and finally Randy, who bent over his wife for a long instant, his sobs betrayed only by the trembling beneath his dark navy suit. Only when my gaze broke free from that tender scene did I behold another, as touching as it was startling. Hilda was on her knees, girdling granddaughter and grandson in a tearful embrace. For a change she said nothing, but pressing the puzzled toddlers to her, she gave the matchless gift of mindfulness.

I doubted my words had shaped much of the sentiment of the moment. Still, my hope seemed well placed that a grandmother's tears might begin to wash clear a path to the unqualified mercy and goodness of God. There could be no higher outcome for the day, indeed for any day, than this.

I have conducted at least one hundred funerals since walking through the valley of the shadow with Rosy, Victoria, and Cynthia. With each passing year, my initial conviction about these matters has steadily strengthened: no other work of pastoral ministry even begins to approach the sacred trust of final words, spoken on behalf of cherished lives lost and declaring God's unwavering intention to redeem them.

FIVE

Singular Spirits

. . . for we are but of yesterday, and we know nothing,
for our days on earth are but a shadow.

Job 8:9

Faith regards tragedy
through the lens of redemption.

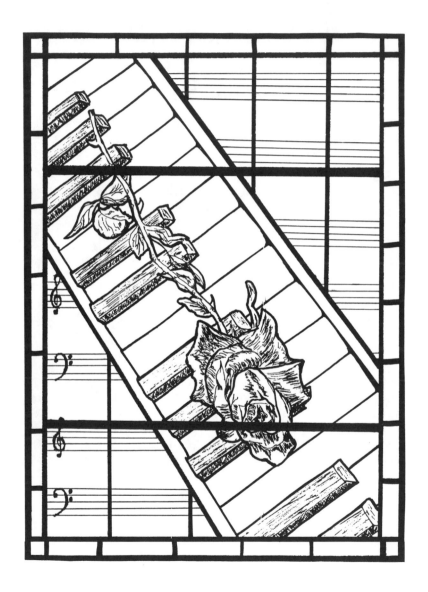

18

Dale

Love Vindicated in Grace

. . . by the grace of God I am what I am. . . .
I Corinthians 15:10

Dale came to us to die. It took an embarrassingly long time
for me to figure this out. Once I did, it seemed more glaringly
obvious than the most elegantly simple utterance of Christian
doctrine ever to start my head nodding in assent. It became a
credo of my pastorate. Sometimes people come to the church
to die.

On the face of it, Dale's arrival made great sense and no
sense whatsoever. He was as staunch a Pentecostal as any whose
arms ever quarreled with gravity in the frenzy of prayer till they
shook hands with the rafters or the Holy Ghost or more likely
both. He had been attending a large apostolic church so far
across town from us it was almost in another time zone. But he
lived near our church. So while I doubted that the Spirit, blow-
ing where it willed through Pentecostal flesh, instructed many of
their number to switch to a *Baptist* church closer to home, I gave
the matter no more than passing thought for his first month in
the pews.

Dale cut a very fine appearance from those pews. His satiny
baritone and winning smile began to earn him the unsolicited
admiration of our single women ages forty to seventy-five. Soon
we learned that he tickled the ivories as ably as he did the
middle-aged women's fancies. This quickly landed him a seat at
the worship keyboard. Every Sunday morning at 10:25 sharp,

Dale serenaded the congregants to their places while the choir and organist launched one final assault on the anthem well out of earshot. His specialty was revival hymnody with all the arpeggiated embellishments over which our seniors had been raised to swoon. Such had been denied them of late due to the more classical tastes of recent ministers, especially myself. They slurped up this musical offering the way a winter-worn gathering mobs the first juicy watermelon of the picnicking season. To deny that Dale gained a place of veneration in the hearts and minds of the faithful would be like calling Calvary a minor blip on the screen of Christian history. Dale brought new life to us.

It was haltingly that Dale invited me into his secret world. He lived in a three-bedroom bungalow, fully appointed and immaculately kept. He lived there alone, but the scale and polish of the place confided that something or someone was missing. We sat on matching loveseats separated by a coffee table with glass top and sleek legs of cast aluminum. Dale owned more Christian tapes and CDs than a gospel radio station. To the sentimental strains of "To God Be the Glory," he told me of his lover's death from AIDS.

When Dale first came to Ashgrove Church, John was not long gone. He had not shared Dale's enthusiasm for "the things of the Spirit," nor had he attended church. They resembled many couples whose discreet upbringings issue in irreconcilable habits and tastes. In rare instances one or the other manages to cross the bar. Most of the time, the best they can hope for is some mutual accommodation. Husband drives wife to Sunday school. Wife polishes husband's bowling ball. Lovers alternate dining preferences on nights out. Dale was born and raised in the church, and so, whatever else he chose or was chosen for him, Dale was destined to die there.

In every other way, Dale and Pentecostalism were a match made in heaven. But, according to the doctrine of his own church, gays were excluded from the dispensation of grace. Dale could no more approach that celestial altar of heaven than exchange wedding vows at the front rail of some church sanctuary back on earth in Indiana. This fact had been reinforced with repetitive zeal by a preacher insensible to the wounding power of his own words. They were intended as armor for the faithful to carry into the world. Instead, they were a dagger, piercing the heart of an otherwise ardent follower of the way. After two years of this, Dale had gone Sunday shopping. He had come to us. It was true that our worship didn't quite sizzle the senses, but neither did anyone get burned alive. Dale made his home with us and his peace with God.

In time, Dale divulged what I had come to fear as imminent. He was HIV positive and had begun to display the first symptoms of full-blown AIDS. Dale was fit and fifty, ruddy of complexion, and retained a full head of hair with as congenial a mix of salt and pepper as age ever cooked up. The manifestations of his illness were thus all the more transparent, even to the ignorant and unsuspecting. Sallow, sunken cheeks, offset by a pronounced jaw line and naturally high cheekbones; brown facial blotching, faint but on the move like the merciless blemishes of puberty; frequent absences from worship, tarnishing a previously unblemished attendance record; hoarseness in the now rare offerings of a once splendid solo voice.

The dawning truth was itself like a cancer, spreading through a church body caught off guard and ill-equipped to respond. People burned up energy trying to mind their own business. It was a case of don't ask, don't tell, a lamentable, ineluctable course for a people on uncharted ground.

Dale was in a nursing home the last time I saw him alive. He had arranged for a small TV on a swivel arm that would bring the picture right up to his straining eyes, by now exploding from their sockets. His breathing was pained and frequently erupted in a violent spell of coughing. He followed intently the animated worship of some electronic church extravaganza, as if he planned to absorb its essence into every vesicle of shriveling skin, like a dried-up sponge dropped in a bucket of water. Just what was being said or sung as I sat quietly by his bed I cannot recall. No doubt it was a message of spiritual power and miracle and some genuine wishful thinking. But these tidings, in all their truth and falsehood, did not matter. Dale had long since breathed in deeply the only message of consequence to a man so reduced by love's scandal: Jesus came to die for Dale. God's own audacious love claimed *him* as son.

One week later, on a Wednesday morning in May, people came. I wouldn't have believed it if I hadn't watched them file in with my own eyes. Suited deacons with conservative ties, innocent youths caught in the web of his charm, elderly couples from another moral universe, and of course the full entourage of his middle-aged women admirers, all victims of Dale's contagion of delight. The whole Baptist, heterosexual kingdom of God, it seemed, came out to the sanctuary Dale had come to call home.

And together the young, the old, the songsters and the screechers, the tone deaf and stone-cold deaf, the humble and the high and mighty, joined in a chorus of "To God Be the Glory." We extolled the God who conquers death and brings to all new life.

19

Ronnie

To Walk a Straight Line

For you have delivered my soul from death,
and my feet from falling,
so that I may walk before God
in the light of life.
Psalm 56:13

It was whopping, white, and round as a cage ball, and it stood on two stringy sticks in a freakish defiance of gravity. I rubbed my eyes and shook my head forcefully as if to chase the specter out of my head, but to no avail. There it was, whatever it was, and at last I concluded I'd spied a snowman in the middle of May. As I drew closer, it appeared "Frosty" was on the move, bobbing up and down in arduous rhythm. Yet, in that way of human perception so beholden to the subtlest changes in perspective, by the time I overtook my phantom snowman, all trace of him had melted away. In his place was a ponderous white plastic bag, bursting with beer and soda cans. Gripping the bag was a big black hand extended over one shoulder, while down below stretched a pair of long, spindly legs in tight black jeans. All at once, my heart and mind leapt in tandem, one with feeling and the other with a sudden spark of insight. I knew this man, didn't I—this long-legged man with a thousand cans, whose name I remembered to be Ronnie?

Thoughts of a former time flooded in with the speed of water escaping a broken dam. We imagine we have settled things once and for all, that a clean break with the past is either

prudent or practicable. But yesterday is tomorrow's stowaway. It
hides in the shadows until, all at once, it steps forth to reclaim a
place in the affairs of the present.

While in seminary in the early '80s, I fulfilled an inner-city
internship at a local Episcopal church. The rector was a white
southern Indianian, but the parish was the historic black congregation of the Indianapolis diocese. It was situated on the near
west side of Indianapolis, in the very heart of one of the historic
centers of African-American culture known as Indiana Avenue.
"The Avenue" was celebrated especially for having been, earlier
in the century, a Midwest jazz mecca, featuring the funky sophis-
tication of such notables as the Ink Spots and Wes Montgomery.
The parish was heir to the celebrity of this proud past. Many
members were highly educated and affluent. Most commuted
on Sundays from successfully integrated middle-class neighborhoods to the north, made possible through the desegregating of
housing patterns dating from the 1950s.

By contrast, the neighborhood of the church to which I
arrived in 1981 had declined into a skid row, a sorry blight on the
map of Indianapolis's downtown. "The Avenue" had become
the dilapidated backdrop for numbers running, drug dealing,
substance abuse, and murder. Men lived bottle to mouth—
homeless, hapless, and hopeless. Church members expressed
openly their embarrassment for their reprobate neighbors on
"the Avenue," shaming the environs of the parish, the ground
of a past they revered.

I, meanwhile, had arrived fresh from the cloister of college
life in the shielded serenity of a small Midwestern city. I was easy
mark, fool luke, and pushover john rolled into one. While by day
I explored in seminary the field of higher biblical criticism, by
night I crossed the hermeneutical bridge to the real fleshed-out
world of the gospel—down on "the Avenue."

Shortly after my arrival, the church initiated a food pantry
to feed the neighborhood hungry. Scores of homeless men
queued up at the church door. They lugged bag after bag of
groceries from the church's undercroft out to the street. Then
they emptied their contents and set them on makeshift tables
along inner-city sidewalks, selling them bargain-basement cheap
for booze money. The beat patrol had come to us with the bad
news. Members were flabbergasted.

"Well, if the food sold, then it would be eaten!" I had
reasoned, but this view had not prevailed. Soon we opted for a

food-delivery program, targeting the elderly poor, whose homes reeked of raw sewage and cried out for cockroach stew. Next, we moved into the "repairs on wheels" business, winterizing homes, fixing screen doors, and making toilets flush again. Finally, we began to operate, with the support of the diocese, a temporary shelter for the homeless. These were days of personal anguish, exuberance, and examination. I made many friends, learned several good, hard lessons, and took as tutors some of the unlikeliest souls in the vicinity. Among these was Ronnie.

It had been pure coincidence that I first came across the man with the cans. On a chilly October day, I had just pulled into the church parking lot when, from around the corner of the building, came a towering figure, standing six feet, seven inches tall—nine, counting the skull cap. He was transporting, with long and deliberate strides, a burden of impossible proportion. He halted his gait and studied me intently until I, too, froze in my tracks. Then, in great relief, I realized he was staring not at me, but at the can of Pepsi in my hand.

"You done wit dat, ma man?" he said.

Without answering, I swigged down the remaining half a can and pressed it into his free hand. He crushed it down flat and tucked it into his belt.

"Hi, I'm Wyatt Watkins," I said. "I work here at the church."

"Name's Ronnie," he said.

Ronnie was lanky but muscular in build. His beard was a stubble and his hair a frazzled 'Fro. Though he had been walking the streets all through the night, he had an animated mien that seemed to say either, "Been drinkin'," or, "Need to be drinkin'," but as to which of these held I was a lousy judge. His feet were clad in black army surplus boots. Their soles were slightly worn on the insides, but they had a lot of walking and kicking left in them. Essentially tongue-tied, I managed a few doltish questions with a sober blend of curiosity and apprehension—how did he manage to find all those cans, how long did it take him, where did he dispose of them, and so on. Ronnie seemed all too happy to indulge my inquisitiveness, and this went a long way toward putting us both at ease.

Ronnie made a living out of aluminum can collection. He had long since pinned the endeavor down to a science. His very existence, in fact, was predicated on an elemental methodology of survival. He had no family, held no job, and owned no home. He lived on the streets with two simple needs: money and

money—some for a subsistence diet and a good bit more for
drink. These requirements satisfied, Ronnie could live to walk
another day. And walking was his life. A salvage business on the
cutting edge of the recycling boom was buying aluminum at ten
cans a penny. If Ronnie could haul a few thousand aluminum
cylinders each day, he would survive. In Ronnie's case, it would
have been truer to say each night. He adopted the third shift,
having determined that the best way to rustle cans was to beat
the competition to the dumpsters behind every restaurant, bar
and night club on the west side. Ronnie was good at this—in
fact, he was the very best at what he did, and he knew it.

Ronnie slept during the day. It might be on a park bench,
down a dark alley, or in the grass under a blazing sun. It mattered
little, because what he brought to sleep was the sweet solace of
total intoxication, the creaturely comfort of a thousand woolly
sheep racing through his blood stream, cloaking the tragic truth
of his life beneath a sweet fleece of delusion. This was Ronnie's
existence. He possessed neither past nor future, but lived in the
limbo of a perpetual present with his single passion—a sacra-
mental affair with *spiritus frumenti*. His was truly the religion of
ultimate self-sacrifice. While pathetic, Ronnie's story possessed a
poignant strength. It displayed vividly life's stubbornness, the
drive to survive at all costs. The effect on me both of tale and
teller was profound.

Following our first encounter, I saw Ronnie often, usually
on the street, heaving his bundle from ditch to dumpster. Then,
in the dead of winter, he began to stay on occasion in the shelter
of the church's undercroft. Folding cots were supplemented by
old pews on high-census nights. Wool blankets were provided.
One or two volunteers would stay the night as well and make
breakfast for our guests in the morning. The shelter was vacated
by 8:00 A.M. Blankets were draped open and sprayed down with
Lysol in preparation for the night to come.

Spring arrived, and we saw Ronnie less frequently. Weeks
would pass without the first sign of him. I would come to fear the
worst when, quite suddenly, he would reappear. Some Sundays
during worship I would spot him in the back, having sneaked in
late to await the service's conclusion, when he might receive a
bite to eat and shoot a little bull. As long as he was reasonably
sober, he had been welcomed. Then, in late summer, Ronnie by
chance entered the sanctuary during my monthly moment for
mission. I was promoting the annual Church World Service Crop
Walk for world hunger. That year, there were to be four separate

walks, originating ten miles out from the city's center on the north, south, east, and west sides. From four gathering points, walkers would start at the same hour and converge on the downtown simultaneously. Sign-up forms and pledge sheets were in the back, I had announced. All one needed were sponsors and determined legs.

Ronnie's ears had perked up at this last part. In the middle of the Eucharist, he went to the table and picked up a pledge sheet. After worship, he had made a general announcement. He, Ronnie Kemp, would be walking. He had his sheet. He was looking for pledges. With his legs, he would fight hunger. "Walkin' for hunger," he had said, "that's what I do every day!"

Walking for hunger or for any other cause was a notion foreign to the experience of the congregation at large. In the end, only my wife, Donna, and I—and Ronnie, of course—had volunteered. The walk was scheduled for a Saturday morning. Donna and I had opted to start on the north side, as the gathering point was the First Baptist Church. We left at the first indication of dawn. Our plan was to meet Ronnie at the church and take him out for a hearty breakfast. But upon our arrival, Ronnie was nowhere to be found. For the two weeks prior, he had journeyed often to and from the church, collecting pledges in his jivin', fun-lovin' way. As early as the Wednesday evening prayer service that week, he and I had checked signals. Now, when it counted, Ronnie was a no-show. Donna and I knew pretty well what this meant. We began driving up and down the side streets, searching behind abandoned buildings. We even commenced checking the dumpsters ourselves. Finally, we halted the search and headed north up West Street, keeping eyes open all the while for that macabre dance of man and bottle.

Vigilance paid a dividend on the corner of West and Twenty-fifth Street, on the curb under the fading light of a street lamp. Ronnie had passed out perhaps hours before. He was just beginning to stir, the artificial warmth of the night's spirits having worn away in the early-morning chill. We parked around the corner and approached him with our perfunctory stares of exasperated judgment. These were only in part due to any justified sense of indignation. They were equally reflections on our own ignorance of the tangled web of cause and effect lying there personified on cold concrete.

Ronnie grew immediately defensive. What did we want, and what were we thinking, and why was it our business?—which of course it wasn't. But the matter at hand remained. Did he want to walk, and would he be able to make it, and what could we do to help?

"I need coffee," he said. "I'm doin' the walk! Jus' get me *coffee!*"

By 8:30 A.M. we were leaving First Baptist Church in a procession of thousands. The throng was largely white, with many elderly and a large number of young couples navigating strollers across busy streets, over curbs, and around every obstacle. Donna and I were hoping just to blend in, but Ronnie was already putting on a show. He could walk circles around these tenderfoots, and they were going to be sure to hear about it. He would begin to move his gangly legs at so fast a clip that Donna and I could barely keep up. Somewhere ahead of us, he would attach himself to some group of unwitting walkers and annoy them to the point of provocation. Then, at last, he would circle back to our place in the procession, where I once again would ask him please to walk with us at our own sorry pace. Ronnie would scoff, and then off again he would traipse.

But as the morning wore on, and as the haze cleared, both Ronnie's and the sky's, and as the sun grew hot, things began to change. Ronnie ceased his frolicking sideshow. Fatigue and morning coffee conspired to calm Ronnie's nerves, and he began to focus on the real undertaking of the day. Slowly it seemed to dawn on him just what this was in which he had come to participate. He was walking—yes, just as he always was—but, that day, he was doing it for world hunger. He was walking for others, walking for the world—for people just like him in places everywhere. The Crop Walk posters, the checkpoints, the well-wishers, the friendly honks of motorists, all began to work on Ronnie, until he assumed an unprecedented sobriety of purpose. People began to take note of this tall, dark figure, a raised beacon on a sea of slow-moving legs.

It was then that the miraculous happened, that a path was cleared for the arrival of a thing of rare beauty. At around the halfway point of the walk, we came upon a middle-aged woman in a wheelchair. She was pushed by a female companion who showed signs of growing languor. They had been among the very first to embark on the walk, hoping to beat the heat to our downtown destination. But progress had been slow, and the wheelchair operator had taken to stopping at every corner to catch her breath and rest her weary arms and legs. Striding confidently onto the scene was Ronnie. I watched as he sized things up, recalling how I, likewise, had once been so appraised. In an instant, Ronnie had put a kindly arm around the haggard helper and relieved her of her burden. Then, at a leisurely pace he began to guide the wheelchair forward toward its goal, all the while speaking reassuringly to the woman who had so unsuspectingly fallen into the lap of his care.

The five of us continued on down College Avenue, then west to Meridian Street, with Ronnie at the controls. With every step, every revolution of the wheels, Ronnie took us nearer the heart of the city, ever deeper into the downtown—into Ronnie's world. At long last, we arrived at the mall of the War Memorial, a curiously fitting site to celebrate peace waged through a day's battle against hunger. Suddenly, Ronnie had turned, as if to present himself to us, triumphant.

"Yeh scc! I walked circles 'round ya'll!" is what Ronnie might have said on an ordinary day of normal happenstance. Instead, Ronnie had smiled his biggest smile and bid the ladies a polite farewell. The woman in the wheelchair had held Ronnie's hand and pulled him down for an affectionate hug. From there, we had bled in among the sprawling masses of aching feet. We ate hot dogs, drank lemonade, and joined in renditions of folk gospel favorites. Church vans and buses arrived to transport us back to points of origin. Meanwhile, Ronnie had slipped away, unnoticed. His body exhausted, he must have craved sleep. More likely, the habit of the ages had been sounding its compelling call, drawing Ronnie down again, into that darksome underworld of psychotropic tranquility.

Sadly, we saw little of Ronnie through the balance of that year. I had collected his pledges myself from disbelieving parishioners, forced to take our word for it that Ronnie had walked the walk. Indeed, from around Forty-second Street to the Meridian Street mall, Ronnie had walked the straightest line of his life. More than that, he had forged for himself a place of enduring fondness in at least four hearts. These in turn served as symbols, I believe, of that day's deeper journey—downtown, onto "the Avenue" of God's eternally loving, redeeming heart. In late spring of the next year I left the church, taking with me enough recollections to last a lifetime, none more vivid than the memory of the straight-walking, jive-talking man with the cans.

Back out on the county line, west, fifteen miles and half a decade distant, I pulled alongside my friend on foot and had a look. It was immediately evident that I had been mistaken. This was not Ronnie. This was a younger man, not as tall, with better teeth, smoother cheeks, and more white in the whites of his eyes. This was not my Ronnie. Ronnie might still be "out there" somewhere, but here was the next generation can man, the *nouveau pauvre,* the prevailing citizen of the street, who had already left Ronnie figuratively if not literally in the dust.

"Where you headed?" I asked him, rolling down my window and leaning out.

"The recycle," he said. "Up there." He pointed up the road, but there was nothing visible on the horizon, only corn and beans, beans and corn.

"Need a lift there?" I asked. I had offered this with uncertainty as to whether I could even deliver, given the enormity of his burden.

"No thanks, man," he said. "I can walk. It's what I do."

"I can see that!" I said.

Then I remembered my morning Pepsi. His bag was torn slightly at one point near the top. I took a last swig, crunched the can down, and tossed it in.

"OK, man," he said in thanks.

"You take care," I ended.

"All right, then."

As I pulled away from him, I looked back through the rearview mirror and meditated on the miraculous gift of strong legs and sure feet. To be led well by them was the essence of hope, and behind such hope one might always discover the gracious and unrelenting presence of God.

20

Heath

A Free Spirit's Release

For all who are led by the Spirit of God are children of God. For you did not receive a spirit of slavery to fall back into fear, but you have received a spirit of adoption. When we cry, "Abba! Father!" it is that very Spirit bearing witness with our spirit that we are children of God, and if children, then heirs, heirs of God and joint heirs with Christ—if, in fact, we suffer with him so that we may also be glorified with him.
Romans 8:14–17

The avenues were few by which teenage youth came to Ashgrove Church. Over the course of my ministry, we had welcomed several young families who had moved to the outskirts of town, but in those instances the children were quite young. From time to time, adult congregants brought along youth from their own neighborhoods or next of kin. These, too, tended to be younger children, eager for that showering of attention and affection that is the special province of Sunday church school and its teachers.

As for the handful of children reared at the little church in the grove, by the time they reached the ninth grade, they had already surpassed many of the time-honored milestones of teen development. These included taking their parents for granted, resenting their families of birth, and plotting the deaths of their younger siblings. Most had grown indifferent by then to anything older than the tennis shoes on their feet—speaking for the male gender at least. They wished for nothing except to wear Nikes and to be with kids their own age at least twenty-four hours a day, and a little church like Ashgrove was the last place on earth they were inclined to look for either.

After sweet sixteen, all bets were off at any rate. This was the magic, tragic age of the minimum-wage job required to earn money for a car. All too often, it was also the first opportunity to drop out of school in order to work full time and get behind the wheel all the sooner. This required their parents' permission, of course, which was granted far more often than one would like to think. With free public education in jeopardy, what real chance did bonfires and Bible trivia quizzes stand?

My attempt to resuscitate the youth group was understandably a nonstarter. If it only took a spark to get a fire going, then, at the conclusion of my efforts, the entire county should have been burned down to embers. Instead, youth ministry at Ashgrove Church was as inflammable as asbestos and arguably as unpromising for our long-term health.

It was all the more unusual, then, that a down-and-out mother and her delinquent son wound their way over ten miles of city street, airport tarmac, and cornfield to our address. On a chilly Wednesday in March, Glenda Blaine urged her dilapidated Dodge Dart into the drive of the church. It was a scuttle of rust, with no excuse for not having kicked the bucket many heaps in the scrap yard earlier. The clanky lifters of its slant six made it the biggest knock-knock joke on wheels. Glenda tramped to the church door with the tenacity of a bill collector who has resolved this time around not to be turned away empty-handed. Back in the car, suffering from acute ennui, was her sixteen-year-old son, Heath, the unenthusiastic theme of her mission in earnest.

Heath was on probation by order of the juvenile court for truancy and the verbal abuse of a teacher and a principal. He was tall and stringy as asparagus, bright and quick, with an uncanny gift for recalling detail. Heath loved to draw. His assignment notebooks were filled with comical caricatures of former teachers, teen antagonists, and his mother's old boyfriends. His razor-sharp wit cut up anyone who stood in his way—or at least it would have if teenagers were accustomed to fighting with words only. Heath had suffered mercilessly at the hands of huskier boys. He always managed to carry his banter one clever comment beyond discretion. Bullies had postulated that it would take a big fat lip to put a stopper in it, and they were delighted each time he confirmed their hypothesis. It was their only excursion into scientific inquiry.

With each passing year, Heath's situation had grown more grave. No one had the time or the patience for the chicanery of an emotionally crippled adolescent. He ceased looking for trouble and became it. At last, after a back-row paper-wad throwing episode in which Heath had been singled out for disciplinary action, something inside him had come unglued. Heath had said things to his teacher that could never be retracted. When encouraged to confess his transgression in the principal's presence, Heath had been more than glad to repeat his remarks verbatim. For this he had been awarded a handcuffed escort to juvenile jail and an indefinite suspension from the ninth grade.

Heath's court appearance had pitted the impersonal face of the justice system against the painfully personal side of a dysfunctional family system. His mother had arrived in a skimpy cocktail dress and bared her soul, along with other things, before the court. By the time the presiding judge had convinced Glenda to contain herself or be cited for contempt, he was full of pity for any child in her care. Heath was ordered to perform forty hours of community service within sixty days, assigned a probation officer, and released somewhat reluctantly into the custody of his own home.

Heath lived with his mother, his younger half-brother, Joey, and Glenda's latest liaison. They resided in a Section 8 apartment house on the near south side of the city. Glenda subsisted on institutional compassion in the form of a monthly AFDC check. Her live-in boyfriend subsisted on the misguided passions of Glenda herself. He was the self-avowed victim of a chronic back injury suffered in the army, and he self-medicated every hour on the hour and often in between. Glenda got hitched to losers the way a bomb squad courts peril. What few motherly instincts she possessed were squandered on children living in adult bodies, while the real little lives under her protection languished.

Predictably, Glenda and Heath had frittered away the first six of the eight weeks allotted by the judge, failing to follow up on any of the court-provided community service leads. Meanwhile, Heath had been sleeping late into the afternoon and violating the house-arrest rule with impunity. He had been hanging out at several friends' homes or on the street till all hours of the night. Only the combination of well-delivered threats from the probation officer and some unbidden sense of either the heaven or hell within—more than likely both—had wrested Glenda from idleness. She had rounded up Heath, revved up the Dodge, and turned westward the wheel of fortune, stopping at every church in her path. After a five-hour steeple chase, she had finally arrived at the county's edge.

"No church between home and here was willin' to lift a finger to help," she claimed, "except to thumb their noses! After you, I don't know where to go, 'cause the road kinda runs out!"

Glenda had a good point. The court required her son to accrue his community service hours within the county. Glenda's haggard appearance indicated she had walked many roads right down to the last ditch. This trip had all the makings of just one more futile trek down the bitter lane to oblivion. It was undeniable that the ditch at the end of this trail was Ashgrove Baptist Church.

I promised Glenda we would look around and see what there might be for her son to do. Then I braved the March chill to have a word with him myself. Heath was supine in the backseat of the car. His feet were kicked up and stuffed into the back window, his eyes tightly shut, and the space between his ears engulfed in the sound of a Walkman. The audible strains of punk rock signaled the simultaneous frying of brains and eardrums. After knocking on the window to no avail, I opened the back door and tapped his shoulder. This gave Heath such a violent start that the whole car began to rock and roll. I took this to be a hopeful sign. He might have been angry, embittered and confused, but Heath seemed far from hardened. In fact, he was a sensitive soul with a strong and malleable mind.

Heath sat up and calmed down, and I introduced myself, explaining that I wished to help him. However, I would need his cooperation. What did he enjoy doing? Were there things he was particularly good at?

"Hmmm," Heath said. He rolled his eyes upward in that peculiar way of young people, as if the answer were on the ceiling.

"I can draw," he said at length.

Heath said little else, but I had the strong sense that the gears were engaged and the wheels were turning. Over the short time I was to know Heath, that impression only strengthened.

There was a clear opportunity here. It was conceivable—something good might come of this.

On the pretext that they had no telephone, I asked them to come back to the church on Sunday morning. By then I would have in place a plan for Heath to earn his hours, and I could introduce him to anyone with whom he might be working.

"Sunday school starts at 9:30," I stated. "Worship follows at 10:30. We'd love to see you for either one!"

"Oh, we'll be here, sir!" said Glenda.

I had been tempted to say more, to launch into a long discussion of God, Christ, and church, to issue the sweeping call to repentance and pronouncement of forgiveness, to see them both made whole on the spot. But faith arises contextually, I had come to believe. Word and deed, witness and experience, cohere like bricks and mortar. One builds upon the other; neither builds out of turn. By God's patient forbearance, the process of salvation might commence. Without it, redemption was a pipe dream. Glenda started the car on the third try and sputtered away, maybe forever, but maybe not.

Sunday morning arrived. I hovered around the vestibule, listening intently for the Dodge version of cardiac arrest. The only annoying rattle of motors, however, came from the church's heat pump, battling to hold the building at a toasty seventy degrees, and the occasional jet airplane, angling above the church for a Sunday morning landing. My thoughts turned to that strange reaction of our hearts to things that unfold exactly as we have predicted—things like Heath and Glenda's absence that Sunday. Though I was not in the least surprised, I was still profoundly disappointed.

Halfway into the morning service, an usher opened the sanctuary door and motioned Heath to a seat in the back. His mother had dropped him off with instructions to find a ride home. He was dressed in the identical jeans, T-shirt, and tennis shoes of the previous Wednesday. Just as he was seated, the offering was collected. While I considered this regrettable timing, it also occurred to me that Heath's nearly miraculous presence there was itself the greatest offering of the day. If tithes and offerings were emblems of self-giving, then perhaps simply by showing up Heath had done his part.

During my sermon, I felt more than a little like a self-conscious teenager. At several points, I caught myself wondering whether Heath would regard my talk as the worst kind of classroom lecture, suitable only for dozing or doodling. I was preaching a Lenten message from Mark's Gospel, the eighth and ninth chapters. This was the turning point of the whole account. Jesus was shifting his enormous life energies in the direction of his death. Resolutely he faced Jerusalem, where he would confront all the powers of darkness. A warrior chief was applying his war paint, but it was administered in the shape of a cross. The battle to be waged and won was of Jesus' passion, his loving, self-giving sacrifice. "The Son of Man is to be betrayed into human hands, and they will kill him. . . ."

Moreover, Jesus invited his disciples to deny themselves, take up their crosses, and follow him. They must wear the war paint of love and sacrifice as well. But such crosses were not to be equated with the incidental hardships and inconveniences of a given day. They entailed the life-and-death struggles for ultimate meaning, purpose and destiny. And, through such struggles, we too are yoked with Christ in his universal work of redemption. There are some standing here today, Jesus said, "who will not taste death until they see that the kingdom of God has come with power."

Following worship, Heath remained shyly in the pew. From there he was graciously greeted by many worshipers, nearly all of them five times his age. Harold Hatch was first to reach him. I had already asked Harold to assist Heath with the first phase of his community service. He had chosen a scraping and painting project, weather permitting, on the neglected north side of the church. In addition to learning from a paint-slinger par excellence, Heath could only benefit from Harold's sage wisdom. Harold would take him to school in the lessons of painting and life. Within moments, they had taken to each other like bare wood and a bonding primer.

Harriet Crabtree shook his hand and coughed, a sure sign of her full regard. Sarge Grimshaw, the chairman of the trustees, whom I had duly alerted to my plans, studied Heath's long hair like a tree surgeon counting up dead limbs one at a time. Heath and crazy Heidi Hapness simply looked at each other and began to laugh—two souls stuck on precisely the same outlandish frequency. Harold, Heath, and I met briefly to plot out details. Then Harold and his wife, Gladys, gave Heath a lift across town to his home.

On the first acceptable day, Harold picked up Heath around the hour of the morning Heath had grown accustomed to turning in. He only had to honk the horn twice. The air at dawn was brisk, but temperatures soon climbed into the low sixties. All morning they scraped and caulked weather-beaten clapboards. At noon they had lunch under the great oak tree in the south yard. Gladys had fixed double of everything. Harold jawed his way around the world and through the day, occasionally cutting to the marrow of things—the veteran orator at his avuncular best. Heath mostly listened. From time to time he would loosen up to parlay with Harold with lively brilliance. But when it came to really chewing the rag, Harold was in a class by himself. Never before in Heath's life had he enjoyed the undivided attention of a grown man. Three days and nineteen hours of service later, the job was completed. Harold was pleased with the work and, justifiably so, with himself.

"Well, I loosened him up for you, Preacher. Now he ought to be putty in your hands!" remarked the painter-poet.

Phase two, as I saw it, was a double mission project. Heath had become a mission, but this did not preclude his participation in the causes of others. Give a mission to a mission, was the idea. Allow Heath to sink teeth and talent into an elevating endeavor. Provide for him something of greater scope and significance than mere pity for his unprivileged beginning. The object in question was the annual America for Christ campaign of our denomination, by which works of the gospel from evangelism to social justice were sustained. This was my first crack at the America for Christ cause. I knew it to be a hard sell in many church settings like ours. By their own admission, the rank and file of Ashgrove Church were ignorant both of the money trail of mission and its concrete impact on real people and events. Our denomination, the American Baptist Churches, held a hard-earned, middle position between locally autonomous mission endeavor and the coordinated efforts of mission societies supported institutionally by the consent of the churches. The task was to represent the places of Baptist mission in America as vividly as possible, to make them literally jump off the page. My strategy, in a word, was "Heath."

For the better part of a week, Heath and I met to study the campaign and the various missions it supported: ministries among native Americans, college campus ministries, new church planting, evangelism, neighborhood action programs across urban America, and so on. In the process, Heath was exposed to information about the church, the Christian gospel, and the

Scriptures. Then I set him up with poster board, maps, charts, and unlimited art supplies and cut him loose. From time to time, I checked his progress, or he would come to me with questions. By and large, Heath worked on his own. With just two days to spare before the court deadline, both Heath's service hours and his mission masterpiece were completed.

On Palm Sunday, the vestibule took on a different look. Two large easels, standing side by side, supported an enormous display. At the top, in stenciled letters, were the words, *America for Christ.* At the bottom was the goal: $1,000. Filling the space in between was a large map of the United States, vividly punctuated by colorful icons of mission sites from around the country, the kind of artwork one finds on souvenir travel posters. As a work of art, it was far from perfect. The map of the states had some proportional problems. Words were misspelled or overran their boundaries. But the humor and facility of the drawings was sly and unmistakable. It was vintage Heath.

For most of the morning, Heath stood guard for mission, lapping up compliments like water in the desert, sharing mission trivia with anyone willing to listen. The good folks of Ashgrove Church opened their hearts and pocketbooks. The ambitious goal of $1,000 was attained and surpassed. A share of God's kingdom had been present in power. Its standard-bearer had been Heath Blaine, bastard son, ward of juvenile court, child of God.

As in the Gospels, so in life. Palm Sunday is followed by Holy Week. Heath had gone home that day into a war zone. Glenda was busy breaking with another beau, according to her strict, predictable pattern. Substance abuse always worsened during such periods, adding to the volatility. Joey and especially Heath bore the brunt of the anger and hurt. Heath spent much of that week away from the house, making the rounds among his freewheeling friends. I stopped by on Maundy Thursday to deliver to Glenda my record of Heath's community service hours for the juvenile court. The evidence of turmoil was visible at every turn, and it reeked out its potent presence as well. Heath was not at home. Glenda had not seen him. Easter Sunday came and went, with no sign of Heath or word of his whereabouts.

Then, late one evening of the following week, I received a phone call from a hospital social worker. The coarse voice of a heavy smoker, undeniably Glenda's, wailed in the background. Heath had been shot. A crazy man in their neighborhood had done it. Could I come to the county hospital emergency room? Could I come *now?*

The man at the trigger, I learned later, was known as Cord, and he was a loose cannon. By his early twenties, he was already a diagnosed paranoid schizophrenic. Cord heard voices during the day and talked back to them through the night. Lately, he had taken to firing at them into the darkness. He kept a .22-caliber pistol loaded and ready at all times. He even took it with him into the shower, hanging it in a large ziplock bag from a hook on the shower head. For several months, Heath had been escaping to Cord's ramshackle, garage-conversion home. Cord almost always had beer and weed. Heath and his friends had been welcomed and encouraged to indulge themselves. Yet, that week, Heath had merely sought there a refuge from the domestic turmoil of home.

Over the previous weeks, Cord's mind had apparently taken several sizable leaps into the bizarre. He would shut himself into his house for days and open the door to no one. Heath was well aware of the change, but he had made a lifework of defying clear warnings. He would bang on the back door until the noise shook loose Cord's imaginary voices and, once inside, Heath held them at bay with his incomparable wisecrackery, simultaneously charming and crass. At least twice before, Cord had taken pot-shots at Heath's feet, but on this night, destiny took better aim. Perhaps, on this occasion, Heath had not rattled the voices hard enough. Or perhaps Cord's demons, like all the bullies before, had determined finally to put their words into action. But, just after midnight, Cord had snapped determinatively. He had aimed the .22 at Heath's chest and pulled the trigger.

My wife, Donna, who is a nurse, and I had driven like demons to the hospital, but we had been too late. There was never really any hope of survival. The shot had been fired at close range. Heath's spirit must have slipped imperceptibly from his body in the manner of his many free-spirited exits in life. By the time we arrived at the trauma center, the coroner had earned a night's pay. Glenda and Joey were alone in a quiet room. I muttered words of Christian comfort as we hunkered down with them beneath grief's long shadow, but Glenda seemed not to be listening. She was already on a different track, along her essential course of survival: mustering the anger to mask the pain. She vowed that the son of a bitch would pay with his life, one way or another.

Heath's funeral was an awkward affair. It took place at the Fletcher Funeral Home, a converted Italianate with white aluminum siding and green shag carpeting, running wall to paneled wall. There was no separate viewing for Heath, only a two-hour showing prior to a memorial service. When I arrived, family members by and large were either smoking rings around the mortuary entrance or in the coffee lounge, drinking themselves into caffeinated hysteria. Glenda herself was tranquilized but did her level best to introduce me to the family.

Heath's father arrived, but Glenda and he were not on speaking terms. He and his girlfriend excused themselves at some point before the service. Glenda's father was there as well, and it became clear that they, too, had not seen each other or spoken for a number of years. At some point, he had wandered away down the street without explanation. The funeral was delayed while several local establishments were searched, but he could not be found, nor did he return on his own.

In the eulogy, I revisited the text of my Easter sermon, which Heath had not been present to hear. He had been featured prominently therein, his life an illustration of resurrection power, still in potent residue nearly two thousand years after the fact. Surely Heath's death no less than his life bore witness to Easter's truth: Heath was a child of God, an heir with Christ Jesus. God would never let him go! At the cemetery, Glenda made her way to my side and pressed into my hands a notebook. It was Heath's last, retrieved from the scene of the crime. Flipping through it, I beheld the familiar souls and scenes of the church he had just begun to know as family. On his last page of entry was his rendering of Ashgrove Church's pastor.

He had captured my essence unflatteringly, as in the case of all his victims. My eyes were more buggy than I wanted to see, the tip of my nose more rounded, and my jaw line so keen edged he could have sharpened his pencil on it. I was wearing some sort of clerical collar and, right in the middle of my high forehead, Heath had drawn a cross. This must have been his idea of the pastor's war paint, and I was more than a little relieved he had spared me matching ear and nose rings. For an instant, I had thought the collar and cross typically, humorously Heath. Then it had come to me that, here, on the last page of his last notebook, with the last stroke of the lead, Heath had drawn his first and only cross of Christ. It was burned there, quite literally, on my mind. So was Heath, I had realized. Best of all, Heath Blaine himself was burned for all eternity into the heart and the mind of God.

SIX

Sanctified Seasons

Yet he has not left himself without a witness in doing good—
giving you rains from heaven and fruitful seasons,
and filling you with food and your hearts with joy.
Acts 14:17

We script our lives in liberty,
but each successive scene is free playing
its way back to God.

21

Fish Fry

Benevolence under a Big Top

Do not neglect to show hospitality to strangers,
for by doing that some have entertained angels without knowing it.
Hebrews 13:2

Out in the sleepy town of Nebo, Indiana, a few cornfields
west of the county line, resided the Little Big Top Shop, tents
and awnings for rent and purchase. Its owner and founder was
Ed Garrett, longtime trustee at Ashgrove Church. Ed knew awnings. He sewed them in every material, from tarpaulin to nylon
to sailcloth. He stocked every style, from marquees to wigwams,
fly tents to canoe tents, tambus to lean-tos, round tops to rag
tops. But Ed's passion was the big top. In no disrespect to the
snappy shop name his wife, Alice, had dreamed up, the *bigger*
the big top, the better. In Ed's view, anything smaller than a
thirty-by-forty foot canopy was a pup tent.

Ed was a most generous supporter of the Baptist cause. It
was he who had donated the tall teepee tents to Isaac McCoy
Camp, and the soft canopy over the drive of Ashgrove Church
was cut from his best canvas. It was rainproof and sleetproof and
as hailproof as asphalt shingles. The Little Big Top Shop supplied several surrounding municipalities with bunting for Flag
Day and Independence weekend, and whatever was left over
came to Ashgrove Church, where it was displayed with patriotic
panache. And it was from Ed that the church had acquired
the fatefully large American flag that refused to stay up the
flagpole. Twice the pole blew over under the sheer force of 150

wind-flapping pounds. Ed had complained to Sarge Grimshaw that Harold Hatch, who had planted the pole in the first place, couldn't make a toothpick stand upright in a block of concrete. Harold just shook it off, of course, like water beading down moisture-resistant canvas. Even after the post was made secure, the flag's weight and Ed's slick nylon cord conspired to lower the flag appreciably over just a few short days. Regardless of the knot employed—half-hitch, square, sheepshank, sheet bend—the flag seemed determined to fly itself at half-mast. I voiced no opinion on the subject but considered privately whether God might not be calling some Baptists back to their antiestablishment roots.

Ed's primary passion, however, was big tops, especially the one for the annual Ashgrove Baptist Church fish fry. On a blisteringly hot Tuesday in August, Ed arrived in his delivery van with enough awning to sail *Old Ironsides*. He laid it all out on the grass in the church's south yard, just roadside of the large oak, overshadowing the pet cemetery. His crew got right to work, manipulating ropes, stakes, poles, and pulleys with the disciplined rhythm of a yacht racing team. All fifteen tables from the fellowship hall were set up in rows, and folding chairs followed— the church's ninety-six and two dozen more from Jessie Calhoun's Elk Lodge. A rented platform and risers were erected at the tent's south end, and cables were run for a sound system. Finally, Ed took the deep fryer and all the accessories out of mothballs, gave them a good, hard scrubbing, and readied them for use. As always, Ed brought things along so far and no farther. He returned to work and awaited the weekend in an attitude of ambivalence. While eager to reap the reward of his effort in ticket sales and church profits, Ed was equally dubious of the competence of others to play their respective parts.

The fish fry was intended as the big moneymaker of the season, the one opportunity to balance the budget and pay the bills. But, year after year, Ed had seen his impressive initiative frittered away like caviar wasted on cats. Russ would neglect to hang the big "Fish Fry" sign until the week of the event. Posters might be printed but were rarely posted beyond the walls of the vestibule. Sign-up sheets for side-dish donations remained blank until the last minute, making for great surpluses of some items and a scarcity of others. There could be too little greens and collards to scare away small children, but enough baked beans to launch the big top like a gas balloon.

Worst of all was the abysmal quality of entertainment. There were the appearances by the Ashgrove Baptist Choir, numerous and regrettable, during which the carryout line went through the Styrofoam at a furious pace. There was the year the accordion player canceled out—just in the nick of time, as most tell it. In 1978, a stereo was hooked to loudspeakers, volleying sound around the countryside. "Bring Your Own Elvis" nostalgia night was featured on Friday, followed by Bill and Gloria night, in the interest either of contrast or concord, depending upon your point of view. When the bagpipe player came to perform gospel favorites, old man Norris turned his hearing aids off and never turned them on again. Not only did this improve considerably his outlook on life, it was, in all likelihood, the only reason he survived the fish fry of '84. That year, on a particularly infamous evening, Jimmy Grimshaw's steel guitar band showed up, shamelessly shirtless, and blew the toupees off the older crowd. Fortunately, the sound system was itself deep-fried, to grateful applause, only ten minutes into the first set.

So far as Ed was concerned, there was certainly a great spectacle every summer under the big top at Ashgrove Church. But it was no happy sight and turned no pretty profit. Ed was a general with no lieutenants, a lone capitalist lost in a sea of fiscal sloth. Then I matriculated onto the scene, like a new, shiny saber for Ed to rattle.

"Can't you talk to these people?" Ed had asked. "Get 'em fired up about this thing, preach a sermon on it?"

"A sermon on fish fries?" I queried myself.

"When they had gone ashore, they saw a charcoal fire there, with fish on it, and bread. . . . Jesus said to them, 'Come and have breakfast. . . .' "

There were possibilities here, but at the moment I was a hound dog following a different scent. Stepping out of the big top for a moment and looking in on things from a dispassionate distance yielded a one-word question: "Why?"

Why was Ashgrove Church in the fish-fry business?

"Baptists don't believe in fund-raisers. We're not like the Catholics, who hold raffles and bingo nights to pay for the church. We don't believe in that sort of thing. The church should be funded out of members' pockets! That's God's way!" In a student pastorate, a friend of mine had heard these words nearly verbatim, as the congregation debated the merits of holding a rummage sale on church property. He had been attempting to remember whether it was written somewhere that God *has* pockets, when the church clerk dug out of *hers* a crumpled list she had been saving and slipped it into his hands. Compiled there were the annual contributions of twenty-five prominent members. After a cursory review, it had been clear to him exactly why the church was holding the debate. Some of those most opposed to rummaging around on church grounds had been throwing yard sale money into the plate. They were tuck-pointing old bricks in the Baptist facade while ignoring its foundation. A profound, historic commitment to the tithe, based upon a biblical gratitude for God's gifts, had strayed into misguided enmity toward Roman Catholics and a falsely pious view of Christian stewardship.

Thankfully, none of this held at Ashgrove. No one seemed in the least concerned about the propriety of such an event. Patchwork quilt sales and fish fries were as natural as cotton and cooking fat, congenial occasions for exchanging both hot gossip and hot food for cold cash. The only debate was about which of these was more to the point. Ed liked the proceeds. Most everyone else preferred the prattle. I, however, was much more interested in the meaning of the ritual itself. What did the whole exercise contribute to the message of the gospel, lived and shared? Now, there was a sermon, and to Ed's great disappointment, I had preached it, only two short days before the big top went up again to clutter the horizon. The fish-fry sign was still down, and the sign-up sheet was still blank. Another golden opportunity had been squandered. All was lost for another year, and to Ed, I had been no help whatsoever.

Instead, I had fingered back to the book of Genesis, chapter 18, to recall the strange visitation to Abraham by the oaks of Mamre. Was it God who had come to rest there, at the entrance to Abraham's tent, or just three hungry travelers? The text seemed artfully vague. Finally, did it really matter? Did not the practice of hospitality to strangers always invoke the presence of a hospitable God? Abraham offered meat and drink, bread and shelter, and he and Sarah each were filled with the divine presence—she even in a swollen-with-Isaac sort of way. Could not our little ritual of big top hospitality, out on the lonely county road, summon the same? Yes, the church welcomed paying customers, but what they received for a mere pittance was more than a feast. They were invited into the mystical fellowship of believers, offered fish from the body of Christ, himself. Maybe here was a high purpose rivaling even the stature of a big top tent—if, that is, anyone were open to consider such a thing. Predictably, I had received virtually no feedback from my remarks. Those with whom I made eye contact smiled affably.

"See yeh at the fish fry, Preacher!" the custodian, Russ Ingersol, had yammered. "If it's really *you*, that is!" he appended, visibly amused with himself.

"Well," I rejoined halfheartedly, "you never know who might show up!"—portentous words, if ever such were spoken.

It was on that Saturday evening, under a foreboding sky, that they came. The fish fry, day two, was in full and customarily clumsy swing. They approached with the roar of apocalyptic horsemen, saddled on hogs whose roar bested the heavens' growing thunder. Twenty-two gleaming halogen headlights pierced the blackened sky. Turning into the gravel drive of Ashgrove Church in tight formation, they resembled a gaggle of geese, or the Blue Devils in a demonstration flight. Yet they answered to the name *angels*, though they were not riders of God. They were the horsemen of Harley, big, bad, burly bikers from hell, or at least from out of town. They cut engines and parked en masse on the grass, then ambled up to the ticket table like outlaws on Dodge City's Main Street. They might have been tough customers, but, to the relief of all, they turned out to be the paying sort as well. It was amateur night, which at that very moment was clearly evidenced by Chuck Grayson's performance of his three-tune harmonica repertoire. Yet the bikers appeared both amused and genuinely approving. Then, in the very instant they began to pull up chairs backwards around three vacant tables, the rain began to fall in a thunderous torrent, and genius struck the otherwise feeble mind of Heidi Hapness.

While heaping their plates, she had been eyeing with naive fascination the tattoos on the four biker babes. When she saw one of them react to the storm by stealing a nervous glance at the bikes in the grass, Heidi had asked in her inimitably innocent fashion, "Somethin' wrong, ma'am?"

"It don't start good 'n the rain," the woman explained, "and my things is gonna get real wet!"

"Well," Heidi continued, "you'd be more than welcome just to bring them inside the tent here, if you'd like—you know, till the rain dies down a bit, after while. . . ." Heidi looked

inquiringly at Ed. The biker woman consulted a 300-pound—
not counting the beard—black-leather-clad road warrior as the
rain pounded down and patrons dashed to their cars.

"Ssssure," agreed Ed spasmodically.

"No problem," said Harold, taking up the cause. "We can
just push some tables together in here, and make you plenty of
room!"

"Looks like the show's over anyway," I chimed in. "It could
be raining awhile."

The big biker, whose name naturally was Tiny, and his bud-
dies voiced their thanks and began to wheel in cycles while
several of us took down a half-dozen tables and pushed others
together toward the back. Meanwhile, the Ashgrove crowd was
making its way toward the shelter of the fellowship hall. As Heidi
finished filling the bikers' orders, she did something truly in
keeping with her free-handed nature. She invited all of them
into the church, where, she was certain, they would be warm and
dry and enjoy their food "lots more than out here in the stinkin'
rain."

It was clear to me and Harold, and especially to entrepre-
neurial Ed, that there was no way on God's earth even these
bikers would be able to resist Heidi's earnest entreaty. We were
so certain of it that, even before they started gathering up their
cups and plates, we were transporting three tables and a couple
dozen chairs to the fellowship hall. Within another fifteen minutes, there was assembled within the confines of Ashgrove
Church the most unlikely congregation ever witnessed. Other
than the firm no-smoking request, all conversation was remarkably amicable. Harold was perfectly charming. Sarge swapped war
stories with several vets. Ed was appropriately quiet, while Heidi
was emboldened to ask that brand of ridiculous question that so
thoroughly loosened up a crowd and endeared her to all. I
attempted to act natural, but, being by then identified as the
pastor, I naturally failed.

Within an hour or so, the storm had moved on, and the
bikers were preparing to do the same. We showed them the
sanctuary and gave out three pew Bibles upon request. Tiny had
the last word, commenting, "I always said light'n' ou'd strike if
I was to step inside a' one a' these. . . . Came pert' close! . . . See
all the trouble I caused you folks?"

"It was no trouble at all!" we assured him.

"By the way," Tiny added, "noticed yer flag flyin' out there at half-mast . . . Somebody die?"

No one, especially Ed, could muster a word in answer.

"Anyways," Tiny concluded, with genuine feeling, "sorry fer yer loss."

As they roared away, it seemed more than evident they were taking along with them some small portion at least of that most mystical host, freely offered to all by the great Fisher of men himself. I am certain that Heidi and others felt the same. And Ed, who wasn't yet sure just what to think, had at least another whole year to figure it out.

22

Grass-Cutting Days

Seven Hours to Flatland

You crown the year with your bounty;
your wagon tracks overflow with richness.
The pastures of the wilderness overflow,
the hills gird themselves with joy,
the meadows clothe themselves with flocks,
the valleys deck themselves with grain,
they shout and sing together for joy.
Psalm 65:11–13

It took three mowers seven hours to cut the seven acres of land at Ashgrove Church. While these numbers were rounded off, this had been done in a biblically consequential manner, and they had long since been taken to be more or less the truth. The upshot of this was that on Saturdays between 7:00 A.M. and afternoon softball, the church grounds had to be converted to flatland.

For a time, Russ Ingersol, as custodians before him, cut most of the acreage himself. But the trustees worried he was disregarding his other duties, that the church building itself was suffering neglect. So Sarge Grimshaw, trustee chairman, had devised a Saturday grass-mowing rotation, on which he did not fail to schedule every trustee, including the two women board members.

While all the deacons at Ashgrove were males by constitutional mandate, women were elected from time to time to the

159

trustee board—especially older ones with a reputation for clear, common-sense thinking.

"Women's gotta keep them half-witted men folk in line!" Alberta Rump was fond of repeating, though she was careful to save her greatest disdain for preachers.

But Sarge abhorred the practice and sought every opportunity to lay bare the folly of it.

Harold Hatch's wife, Gladys, was a model trustee. She had handled all the church insurance matters and faithfully taken the minutes at monthly meetings. But Gladys, most everyone was aware, suffered from degeneration of the spine and was a brittle diabetic to boot. She could no more have spent Saturdays behind a push mower than hurl the shot put for the Olympic track and field team. The other female on the board was Hassie Longstreet, a spinster from the deep South who had inherited a pile from her father but none of the sense that earned it. She had moved to Indiana to be nearer her only niece and heir. Hassie's beneficence had netted her a place on the trustee board, but there was little else to commend her inclusion. She had respectfully declined Sarge's "kind offer" to cut grass, just as he knew she would, citing as the chief obstacles her age and gentility. "Putting in barns" had always held for her a great romantic power, though she had not herself spent even one day in the fields. But slicing up grass with a noisy little motor seemed as common as cleaning catfish or plucking chickens. She had also remarked that Briggs and Stratton sounded like some revolting rock and roll band, and she was just dingbatty enough to believe it.

This had left an active lawn brigade of eight men, or enough to cover four Saturdays a month, if Sarge and Kip Quarfarth, the board's vice chairman, were willing to devote every other Saturday to it. The trouble was, they weren't. Kip had a standing date every other weekend with Rod, Reel, and Evinrude, whom he was loath to disappoint. And Sarge, though all too happy to supervise, considered that a squad commander's place was back of the line, steadying his men, not thrusting himself carelessly into enemy fire—but then, for Sarge, everything in life was analogous to war.

As things turned out, personnel was the least of Sarge's worries. The trustees' Saturday battle plan carried one uncomplicated objective: to mow flat anything green that wasn't painted.

If it were green but happened to be flowering, the blooms had better be larger than chicory or dandelions. Otherwise, they would be fairy dust by sundown.

The deaconesses had established several flower beds over the years, both of the annual and perennial variety. They existed in various states of upkeep, delineated only by low borders of clay and plastic edging. Under current rules of engagement, they were cannon fodder. Bert Rump's garden alone was safe from the blade. It was surrounded by knee-high chicken wire. In a simmering rage, she had hauled in a bale of it after Kip had mowed recklessly over one of her rhododendrons. Following the murderous deed, she had swooped down upon him like a duck on a June bug, planting herself so near him they nearly stubbed toes. If she'd been a foot taller, they would have rubbed noses as well. At that juncture, Kip's objective had been simply to keep *his* from getting flattened. Once Bert got her hackles up, the odds of escape were slim to none. She would back you up all the way into the baptistery, if need be, until it appeared the promise of new life would be definitively put to the test. In sum, the great hubbub over mowing rights had nearly escalated into a War of the Roses of a different color.

To top it all off, the lawn mowers in the custodial "office," as Russ called it, were themselves endangered species. They were bottom-of-the-line, 2.5 horsepowered junkers, and had been poorly maintained. Increasingly, Saturdays were becoming futile efforts to conjure a purr from old cats with all nine lives used up.

"For God's sake, we're not magicians, after all!" Phil Simson, resident trustee mechanic, had sized it up. Phil longed for the day when the old, green John Deere tractor had mowed the church yard down to dirt in nothing flat. "We'd even pull a big rake behind it to smooth out the sand on the ball diamond!" he once added wistfully. But Old John had dismembered its last blade of grass in the early '70s and made the journey by flatbed trailer to tractor heaven, or at least to the Ferguson's dilapidated barn a half mile away, which may well have been the same place.

It was early in June and I was just beginning my second year as pastor when Sarge called us to the war room for a strategy briefing. Three dead soldiers lay on the field, never to mow anything down again. The war chest was nearly empty. The troops were demoralized. Minds were as blank as an empty clip cartridge. At last Jessie Calhoun piped up that his Elk Lodge, caught in a similar predicament, had hired someone to mow their acreage for much cheaper than anyone had any right to expect. Ears perked up at the idea.

"Think he's Japanese or Chinese or some such thing," Jessie had explained. "But he done us a fine turn a' work last year!"

Everyone agreed that this option should be explored.

We learned that the lawn man was neither Japanese nor Chinese, but Cambodian. Why there was a Cambodian named Sahm Matak cutting grass for a living in rural Indiana was beyond anyone's comprehension. But no one was surprised to learn that he drove a Kubota. It was said he had endured the killing fields under the Khmer Rouge at the time of the Vietnam War, and that he had lost his entire family in the carnage. He had escaped with his life by sheer courage and fortuity, the story went, but the whole account had the ring of hearsay. True or not, few could have fathomed the utter terror of such a thing, of 2 million people—decent men, women, and children from all walks of life—systematically murdered in a cold-blooded agrarian hell. Over just four short years, they were brought to the fields, humiliated in the fields, and returned to the fields in mass, shallow graves. Here was Hassie's "putting in" the harvest—hold the romance, add the macabre.

Like the American public at large, the members of Ashgrove had interpreted the wider war from their own narrow perspectives. Most had supported it, a handful had not, but all had shared the horror of the daily body count. Several sons and close relatives of members had served in Vietnam, though none had come home in body bags. While, with all America, they had both mourned and decried the dead, it was the American dead who mattered. The war was waged on foreign soil, half a world away. The senseless loss of every person and thing one had ever known was a concept too alien for pity.

The trustees beat the bushes for quotes even remotely competitive with the Cambodian Kubota driver but to no avail. Finally, it all boiled down to cost. Sahm came cheap, twenty dollars a cut cheaper than any other lawn service the trustees could locate. And Sarge could not turn up even the shred of a complaint. Everyone seemed thoroughly satisfied with his work. Sahm Matak was contracted for the season, effective immediately.

His first cutting day was like an audition. Half a dozen members found excuses to be on church property at the crack of dawn. By mid-morning, the turnout rivaled that of the most successful spring-cleaning day on record. Deaconesses, standing sentinel around their little victory gardens, called to mind the metal cutouts of outlaws and innocents on obstacle courses at the police training academy. Billy Burton and Jett Burges hand raked the sand out on the ball diamond. Flo Jimson snipped at weeds and grass between markers at the pet cemetery. And, of course, there was Bert, picketing at her chicken wire like a rooster guarding the henhouse.

I was following this with utter amazement from the north yard of the church when, out on the road, there grew the distinctive sound of diesel pulling cold, hard steel. In the next breath, a bright orange tractor rolled into view, topped by a great, round umbrella of faded yellow cloth. At the controls was a small figure wearing an enormous, broad-brimmed straw hat.

"What the blazes is that?" whooped Bert.

"Looks like a Chinaman's hat!" Sarge exclaimed.

"What yeh mean—up on his head or over the tractor?" asked Kip.

"Yeah," said Sarge.

Sahm made his way up the drive as Sarge and I traipsed over to greet him. He smiled liberally, exposing badly decayed teeth. Though he appeared gaunt and frail, he seemed to carry some inner power, a kind of sage presence all his own and quite distinct from the image of him to which my own idle musings had given shape. He seemed to swiftly size up the situation with quick nods of his head at Sarge's every instructional bark. Then he was off down the picketed path like an equestrian storming the steeplechase.

Sahm snaked his well-oiled Kubota effortlessly around the property, between flower beds, along edges of cornfield, around the bases of the ball diamond and back again home. One inch closer to the rhododendrons, and Sahm might have snipped both the chicken wire and the whiskers off Bert's chin. But he never once overshot. He even rotated the scythe up on its side to trim off rogue branches from a row of overgrown forsythias. Sahm ran the Ashgrove gauntlet to flawless perfection. An hour and a half after he had begun, Sahm was finished. Then, with a broad, vertical wave of his hand, which seemed almost to resemble a blessing, Sahm started down the road of celestial endeavor and, undoubtedly, to his next satisfied customer.

"Guy's good," remarked Kip.

"One fine, clean shave!" added Sarge.

"The man is an artist!" summed up Harold.

After that, the throng fell silent and began to disperse in search of the next spectator event, and with any luck, a less stealthy opponent.

By now, I was enthralled and intrigued. On the next cutting day, the church was deserted, but I had made arrangements to be present. At half-past eight in the morning, the tangerine tractor with canary plume chugged into the drive. I raced from the building, determined to speak with Sahm before he could work his wizardry on wheels and then vanish into the fields, his secrets still as veiled as unshucked corn. Sahm had climbed from his roost, wrench in hand, to make an engine adjustment. When I called to him, it gave him quite a start, but, recognizing me, he broke out in beams all over again. Gone was the straw hat and in its place a baseball cap with the words *Bill's Bait and Tackle*—one more ratchet up on the torque wrench of assimilation.

To my delight, Sahm seemed quite willing, even eager to talk. His command of English was tenuous, but between speech, hand signs, and soul, we made out. He was not living alone after all. His wife had accompanied him to the States, and they were staying in an apartment house at the nearby town of Plainville. Sahm did not own a car, but the Kubota was parked within walking distance of their home, on the frontage of a tree nursery. He had purchased it used after two years of diligent saving. He and his wife had not been in the killing fields, though they lost many friends and family in the butchery. After Phnom Penh fell to the Khmer Rouge in the mid-seventies, Sahm and his wife had fled across the Thai border and eventually made their way to America and a new life. Like most of his kinsmen, Sahm was a farmer. Unlike many, he had worked a large rice plantation, where he had had the use of a tractor.

Sahm thanked me for the opportunity to work for us. "I think your people very . . . interesting," he offered.

"Yes, that's for sure!" I agreed. "They're good, big-hearted people, once you get to know them," I added. To my great surprise, I had uttered these words as if I believed them. Then, to my even greater surprise, it occurred to me that I did.

In Cambodia, Sahm had followed *Theravada* Buddhism, a strict form, prevalent in Southeast Asia. God, per se, was not important in its thought. But, as are many Buddhists, Sahm was receptive to testimonies of other gods and truths. He was full of questions about the Christian God and about Christians themselves—What did we believe? I told him that our God was a God of grace. I had experienced before that *grace* can be a difficult category for devotees of other faiths. "God smiles on us in every moment of every day, as if it were our first," I added. "God forgives us even when we have been very bad."

"Does your God *always* forgive?" he asked.

"Yes," I said, "as long as we receive forgiveness as a gift and with a repentant heart."

"I cannot always forgive," he said.

"I guess I can't either," I concurred.

In America, Sahm had been practicing *Pure Land* Buddhism. He worshiped the god of the pure land, a place of paradise. I asked him if he thought of America as a paradise. He smiled and assured me that it wasn't. "There is no paradise here. Just flat land, big plain, like my home in Cambodia." With that, Sahm climbed back onto the Kubota and commenced making some flatland of his own—not a killing field, but an artful shaping of color and contrast and charm.

It was impossible not to hear Sahm's last words as a metaphor for all he had experienced—a flatland regime on a sea of flatland, of tyranny mingled with rice and bleached bones. Cambodia was no paradise. But neither was America. There was too much flatland everywhere. It was in our suspicion of those different from ourselves. It was the unwillingness to recognize the faith experiences of others, to see only one's own as valid. But flatland meant equally the false assumption that all views, all convictions, all religious stances were equivalent, held equal value, without distinction. Flatland was the tyranny of sameness, whether imposed or implied.

Flatland dictated that all green in a section of earth must be cut to the same height. Flatland decreed that, for distinctions to survive, they would need to be separated by something sharp, like chicken wire, or barbed. The demilitarized zone had been flatland. Communism was flatland. McCarthyism had been flatland as well. War itself was the clash of flatlands. Pogroms, inquisitions, and holocausts were Christianity's flatland legacy. The good people of Ashgrove Church had their seven acres of flatland. The culture at large had an endless prairie of it. In an age of tolerance, American life remained as polarized as ever. Societal sentiments seemed to be flattening out and circling in simultaneously, like flapjacks on the hot griddle of controversy.

But after Sahm, no one at Ashgrove worried much again about flat grass and gardens. Kentucky bluegrass in crew cuts held tangled ivy in high regard, and daffodils smiled down kindly upon clover. It was no paradise. But, here, and in other simple places, where differences came face to face, close enough for the common senses to sniff out truth from falsehood, the open-fisted grace of God might continue to prevail.

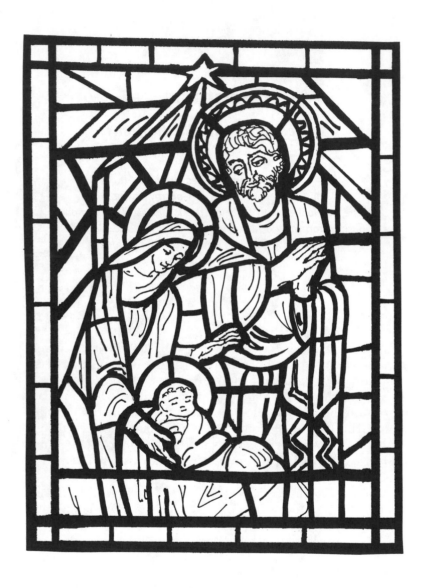

23

Christmas

In Search of the Plastic Jesus

. . . My soul magnifies the Lord,
and my spirit rejoices in God my Savior,
for he has looked with favor on the lowliness of his servant.
Surely, from now on all generations will call me blessed;
for the Mighty One has done great things for me,
and holy is his name.
Luke 1:46–49

On the Saturday after Thanksgiving, as the masses were picking over merchandise left from the greatest sale day of the year, Anna Quarfarth and company were gathering boxes from the storage closet off the fellowship hall and laying them neatly in rows on the vestibule floor. Anna's elves for the day included Jenny Grimshaw, Missy Long, Velma and Harvey's eldest daughter, her sister-in-law, Winona Cox, and, on gopher detail, Anna's husband, Kip. Not just anyone was invited to assist in the meticulous task. Anna was a fussy foreman in the exacting business of decking the December halls of Ashgrove Church for the Season of Light. For the four weeks prior to Christmas, Anna was in all her glory.

The contents of boxes had been carefully labeled. Anna and Kip had purchased nearly all the decorations out of pocket. Anna scoured the Christmas clearance tables each January and kept out a watchful eye over the summer for yard-sale bargains. Each volunteer was given several assignments and told which decorations to take where in order to fulfill them: three Christmas trees along with lights and ornaments; a dozen wreaths with bright red velvet bows, including a giant one for the front door; plastic holly and ivy, to be draped here and there; two candy-striped north poles, a sleigh, and a Nativity scene for the nursery; two illuminated star kits; a table display of a multitude of ceramic angels; several large outdoor displays, which were Kip's department; and two new boxes, which Anna would attend to herself. Missy was given the added assignment of operating the portable tape player. The Quarfarths brought it every year, along with their extensive collection of holiday cassette tapes from the decidedly prosaic end of the spectrum—Christmas with the likes of Bing, Elvis, and the Oakridge Boys.

As Anna's helpers got to their tasks, Anna paced like a school mistress from station to station, straightening, suggesting, correcting, even mildly scolding. Soon a Yuletide parade of light, color, and mood leaped to the eye from every direction. A Christmas potpourri simmered on the kitchen stove. Anna rested her hands on her hips, threw back her head, and breathed in deeply, as if intending to inhale the magic like so much pixie dust. For a change the characteristic sternness of her bearing relaxed its iron grip, as Gene Autry intoned the tidings of comfort and joy Anna had so long awaited.

"Yes," Anna consoled herself, "it's finally come back. We're finally here again. . . ."

Anna and Kip were childless. Throughout her thirties, Anna had marked with envy the journeys of her family and friends through each stage of the parenting drama. She endured their glaring mistakes, breeches of responsibility, and incessant whininess over what seemed to her the only true miracle—a child! To offer one's attention, one's affection, one's time, energy, and devotion, to give one's very life away for one of these would be the most rapturous fate imaginable. But such had not been her portion.

At no other time of year was the sting of childlessness more acute than at the holiday season. Valiantly she had endured them all from a distance—babies' first Christmases, toddlers reaching for their little stockings, the carefully guarded Santa charade, the pursuit of the perfect gift for sons and daughters, and Anna's own musings over that familial inner sanctum known as Christmas morning. Anna had been brave. But Christmas itself had become for her little more than a painful reminder of those elusive joys, and at times it was nearly more than she could bear.

Then, in that way of some events that occur and later defy explanation, Anna Quarfarth had become the "Anna Claus" of Ashgrove. The church had become Anna's Christmastime home, she, a perpetual new mom, and the baby Jesus, her own little bundle of joy.

The centerpiece of Christmas at Ashgrove Church was a Nativity set formed from 100 percent pure hollow plastic. Here was a manger scene for the ages. It featured large, colorful renderings of all invited guests to the scene of incarnation—and even some party bashers! Best of all, it came with a forty-watt lightbulb that slid into a wire clip suspended from the stable rafters, just back of a white plastic star. If you turned it just right, starlight would shine a sharp beam between two rafter joists, down to the manger, and right into Salvation's lap. With the flip of a switch, the star would even blink on and off in rhythm.

"Who knows, maybe the star the three kings follered blinked like that!" Heidi Hapness had suggested one year. "Sometimes I see stars twinkle on and off like that. They even look like they're movin'!"

"Those 'er satellites, not stars!" Kip had corrected.

"Oh. Well, they sure looked like stars to me. . . ."

Setting up the plastic Nativity was the crowning act of a lengthy preparation, and it belonged solely to Anna. Once her elfish assistants were excused from duty for the day, and after Kip positioned the stable just to her liking, added the straw, and clipped on the star, Anna knelt down, as before an altar. From there, she dusted each figurine, three shepherds, three kings, a cow, a goat, a donkey, three sheep—four, counting the one over a shepherd's shoulders—two small-winged cherubs, a drummer boy, an innkeeper, and, of course, the holy family. Ever so tenderly, she welcomed each one into the shelter of the makeshift inn. Next came the manger, padded with bits of straw over a tiny blanket, prepared expressly for this purpose by the Ashgrove quilters. Last of all, was the baby Jesus. Anna lifted him from a small box lined with tissue paper and cradled him in her right arm for a long moment. Then, with the care and precision of a heart surgeon, Anna laid the baby Jesus in the manger. To the observant eye there was little room for doubt: the heart in question was her own.

When first I laid eyes on the plastic Nativity, I fell into a deep funk. There, just inside the door of my church, was the oddest collection of polymerized pilgrims ever assembled. Why a drummer boy and twin cupids? Why kings with crowns, for that matter? And the innkeeper—what was this about, room service? Was there a mail-order catalog? Could you call Dial-a-Figurine toll-free and collect all thirty-eight eyewitnesses at Bethlehem? For four sabbaths in a row and every day in between, each passerby was bombarded by this campaign of misinformation in miniature. In a way, it was a small summary of the season itself.

During those two years already mentioned, which I had spent as a student intern at an Episcopal church, I had visited the other end of the scale of expectancy. Advent hymns were sung to the exclusion of all familiar carols until Christmas day. The only exception was "Joy to the World." This was because "the Lord *is* come" really meant "the Lord *will* come." Therefore, "Let every heart prepare him room. . . ." This premium on inward preparation encompassed the eye as well as the ear. Aside from a bit of tastefully displayed greenery, little decorating was done, certainly nothing as iconic as a manger scene. And if a Christmas tree went up at all, such was reserved for Christmas Eve.

The liturgical year was the Episcopal arena for delayed gratification. In the seasons of Lent and Advent especially, worshipers were hosts making inward preparations for a divine Guest. Easter would revive hearts, but only after the painstaking work of repentance. God would come in Christ at Christmas only after the road of introspection was paved. Without the voice of the prophet Isaiah, Mary's Magnificat, or a sojourn in the desert with John, such preparation was an impossibility. Advent was surrender— not of wallets but of wills. While Episcopalians threw their fat bank rolls into the Christmas shopping ring along with everyone else, here, at least, was a liturgical check on the wholesale consumerism that increasingly was defining the terms of the season.

In many Free Church settings, on the other hand, Christmas, in all its luster, arrived promptly the day after Thanksgiving. At Ashgrove Church, *Advent* read like the work order of a furnace installer. The Christmas season was about preparation the way frozen dinners were about cooking.

After a week with the plastic Jesus, I was ready to act. On the second Sunday of Advent, I tackled the Nativity head-on in a children's sermon entitled "Were You There?" Using a large, wooden manger scene and Luke's Gospel, I took a census of the stable at Bethlehem. The children seemed intent on my words, as I explained which visitors could stay in the stable and which must go. There was no drummer boy there that night, no little angels kneeling inside, no innkeeper and, finally, *no kings!* They were men who studied the stars, and they came a lot later. . . . I concluded that, although these things didn't always happen the way they are sometimes depicted, "The little baby Jesus is still our Jesus, too, because he shows us just how much God really loves us." That, I said, is what mattered.

And all were quiet, children and adults alike, as I placed the manger scene in front of the pulpit with the wise men way off to the side. Even little Sarah Robbins, who routinely wandered off as I spoke, remained attentive.

When Sarah's big brother, Johnny Robbins, got home that afternoon, he ran straight to the manger scene in the living room, and stared hard. "There they are!" he exclaimed. His father, Chuck Robbins, who didn't attend church and who drank too much, was engrossed in an angling show in which a giant walleyed pike was just being reeled in. He motioned Johnny to silence.

"But the preacher said there weren't no three kings, really!"

"Whadoya mean, no kings?"

"Said they weren't *kings,* and there weren't *three* of 'em. That's not in the Bible!"

His father looked perplexed. His wife, Dixie, had purchased the Nativity set for the kids the year before. She'd given too much for it, he recalled.

"Well, looks like three kings to me!" Chuck had said.

"I better take 'em out!" said Johnny, and he proceeded to remove the three men from inside.

"What the. . . ? You put them back in there now, boy!" Chuck had already tied on a couple that morning and was on a short fuse. Johnny hurriedly replaced the kings and left the room.

That evening I received a phone call at home from the chairman of the deacons, Herb Chestnut. He'd been on the phone with Dixie Robbins, and then with a very irate Chuck Robbins, about the manger situation.

"What does that man mean," Chuck had reportedly asked, "tellin' my boy there weren't no three kings? Tellin' him they didn't go see Jesus in the manger! What's he gonna do next, tell my Johnny there ain't no Santa Claus? . . ."

"And others is kindy upset about it, too!" Herb had thrown
in. I talked it over with him briefly, but this was par for the course,
and little I might have said would have made any difference.

In my philosophical struggle with the plastic Jesus and co-
horts, I appeared to have only one ally, Gibson Mayes' stepson,
Brian, and this was arguably worse than no support at all. Brian
was home for the holidays from a junior college. He was seeking
a two-year degree in environmental management. While Brian's
mother, Betty, was proud as punch of the first member of her
family to exceed a twelfth-grade education, Gibson was having a
woeful struggle with the new turn in Brian's thinking. College
always had this effect on young, impressionable minds, Gibson
contended.

All older people had their heads in the sand, Brian countered.

Though they were not blood relations, based upon temper-
ament alone, Brian and Gibson might have been twins.

Since his first day home, Brian had been on a nonstop
tirade against plastics, from the harmful by-products of their
manufacture, to the difficulty disposing of them, to their deleterious effect on sea life. When he got a glimpse of the plastic
Nativity, Brian had a field day. How much pollution was generated by this manger scene? What would Jesus say if he saw
himself in brightly colored plastic? and so on. People were naturally put out by all of this, but they were used to Mayeses who
talked out of turn, and they were doing their level best to get
along in the spirit of the season.

On the third Sunday of Advent, Kip and Anna arrived at the
church early. They had come to unwrap and display thirty
Christmas poinsettias in the sanctuary. I was right behind them,
still hoping for an eleventh-hour rescue of a sermon on the drift.
Anna went first to the manger scene for her Sunday morning
tête-à-tête with the plastic Jesus. All in an instant there came
across her face the look of mortal terror, as if she had just
awakened in the fields to the shout of a heavenly host. Hers was
trepidation that robs speech, because already one's very soul is
shrieking. Kip caught it right away, as did I. We rushed to her
side, bracing ourselves for the sight of just who or what next had
joined the holy family. But we were off by two. The plastic baby
Jesus was gone. Someone had taken Jesus from the manger,
leaving the whole world hovering there over a paltry pile of straw.

Anna crumpled in stunned silence, overcome by a strange
sense of loss, unbidden and bewildering. It was akin to the
feeling she had known and dutifully suppressed each day for the

past twenty years. Just then, it had all come back in a sudden lump sum, a single installment of suffering, like the unrestricted agony of Christ, borne in an instant for a whole fallen and sinful world. Anna was alone. She had always been alone, barren, forsaken. And here was one last pitiable loss, a final, cruel validation of the fact.

Anna's grief quickly solidified to anger, like water molecules in an ice tray, bound to conform to the strict pattern of the cosmos. After a cursory and fruitless search for the plastic Jesus, she had stormed from the church at the mid-point of the Sunday school hour.

"I think she'll be okay," Kip confided, having virtually no grasp of the matter at all.

There were two prime suspects in the crime. No conjectures about guilt were voiced publicly, but they hung palpably in the air, the way frosty breath attests to below-freezing temperatures. Brian had painted a target on his chest with his disparaging comments about plastic. These days, environmentalists would go to any lengths to make a splash about things "no hard-workin' folks could give a care about!" as Sarge Grimshaw had put it.

"Huggin' trees, handcuffed ta chain-link fences—gimme a break!" Jett Burges had mocked.

Maybe he took the Jesus just to make his little point! . . . No one said it out loud, but, as a thought, it had already achieved silent consensus.

The other alleged perpetrator was the preacher. The stir caused by my remarks to the children about the Nativity was far from quieted.

"Why does he have ta take all the fun outta everything! Why can't he leave it alone?" someone had complained. "Who cares who was there in the stable? Could 'a ' been George Washington or Babe Ruth for all I care!"

I knew what some people were thinking, and this only added to my motivation to get to the bottom of things as quickly as possible. Short of stating my innocence outright, I made an impassioned plea from the pulpit for any information leading to the safe return of the baby Jesus to his rightful place in the Ashgrove manger.

Phoning Anna that afternoon, I expressed my regret over the disappearance and restated my sincere appreciation for all her time and effort expended to make Christmas at Ashgrove so memorable. She received my comfort graciously, in the usual way of the grieving.

"It's not the Jesus," Anna assured me. "It's that somebody could . . . *do* this!"

"I know, Anna," I replied. "I understand." And I was thankful at that moment to be her pastor, for I felt certain that I truly did.

The ensuing search uncovered no leads. People were appropriately focused on other tasks. The plastic Jesus would either turn up or it wouldn't. It was only a matter of if and where and when.

The fourth Sunday of Advent arrived. Anna had managed during the week to water the poinsettias, perhaps mingled with her tears, and they appeared happy and contented. With her permission, Gladys Hatch had brought an old baby doll to place in the manger.

In worship, Anna sat calmly on the back pew. When it was time for the children's message, I brought out once again the large wooden stable. This time it was empty, because I was full of hope that I might finally make plain my understanding of the church's beloved Nativity. I had removed every trace of anyone from the company of Jesus in order to bring everyone back again. Everybody and everything in God's world could kneel before the manger at Bethlehem, I had planned to announce. God's love in Jesus had revealed that all are welcomed into the household of faith. We were all of us gathered there at Jesus' feet—the shepherds, the barnyard animals, the wise men, the drummer boy, the cherubs, and all the people of the church, from ninety-four-year-old Earl Norris to little Sarah Robbins. . . .

But Sarah was not coming forward, I noticed. She had been at church for Sunday school. Her mother had dropped her and Johnny off, because, as she put it, "Things is not too good at home just now." Others had noticed Sarah's absence as well. People kept an eye out, because she was always wandering off. A slight commotion in the back indicated a search for her was underway. Then, after a moment, she had been found and was waddling down the aisle, to a growing chorus of shocked surprise. Sarah bore a bundle. It was held tightly in her arms, wrapped in a nursery blanket and had a little pink bonnet on its head. It was the plastic Jesus.

Sarah had been in the storage closet. Emptied for the season of its holiday contents, it had become her latest hideout. Only bare boxes remained there on the floor, and it was down into one of these that Sarah had put the plastic Jesus for a long nap. She had gone to check on him, but, on this occasion, had left the closet door ajar.

When, from the back, Anna realized what was unfolding, she gasped a great audible gasp and started out of her seat. But Sarah was walking now right up to the empty Nativity. She stopped before it and stared. Then she lowered her bundle and pressed it, head first, into the stable. Sarah sat down. The plastic Jesus' feet stuck out of the stable, but she was certain he was home. Anna paced slowly down the aisle. When she arrived at the front and stretched down two trembling hands, it was not with the plastic Jesus that she made contact. It was to little Sarah that she had reached. Anna scooped Sarah up into her arms and carried her away, with her lips to the funny child's face. The children's sermon was over.

After worship, the plastic Jesus was returned, pink bonnet and all, to its plastic crib. Gladys Hatch gave her baby doll to Sarah, who hugged it tightly over her winter coat. Anna held Sarah by the hand and led her out to the car, where Kip waited with Johnny. Anna had phoned Dixie Robbins for permission to take Sarah and John for the afternoon, and Dixie had seemed very thankful. Anna closed the door to the church and, Sarah at her side, skipped out into the crisp air and the day's excitement.

Back in the dark vestibule, the plastic Jesus lay in inanimate calm under the glowing warmth of a forty-watt, intermittent bulb. Its very stillness spoke a silent benediction on the bid of human hearts to breach the gap of loneliness with glad tidings of comfort and joy.

24

Race Sunday

Worship under Yellow

For ye shall not go out with haste, nor go by flight:
for the LORD will go before you;
and the God of Israel will be your reward.
Isaiah 52:12 (KJV)

Jimmy was the picture of glum. Bravado alone carried him from the driver's seat, like a puppet master dangling him from taut strings. His head cocked unnaturally from side to side, and he glanced around as though he did and did not want to be noticed, both at the same time. Jennifer, his wife, sped around the front end of their Ford pickup the way a mother accelerates to the scene of a child's spilled milk. In this case, the child was Jimmy. The milk was morning coffee. It had spilled on all of the places Jimmy was wearing Sunday clothing.

"We was goin' to church fer mercy's sake, Jimbo! Yeh don't have to race a *moron* on a country road on the way to church!" It was clear she would have told the *other* moron the same thing. "After this we're *walkin'* to church in May, Jimmy Grimshaw!"

May was race month in Indianapolis. For a four-week stretch, Indy Car racing ran roughshod over the Circle City, disquieting sleepy streets and addling idle brains—brains like Jimmy's.

Jimmy pressed his bearded chin to his chest, like the Amish at prayer, and stared at his soggy tie. Indeed, these were the moments when he remembered God. Jennifer dabbed mercilessly with a towel at his front side, waiting for him to steal her the slightest glance. On contact, she scowled at him in that way of hers that never failed to purge all residual hot air. When she was satisfied that her dabs and jabs were commensurate with the awful stain of his crime, she huffed into the building, leaving him with his trousers down around his ankles—so to speak!

I greeted her at the church door with the cheeriness of feigned ignorance and then strode out to stand with Jimmy in that strange solidarity of men, who, for all their differences, still put their pants on the same way. At the moment, Jimmy happened to be yanking his favorite polyester tie from around his neck like a broken leash. It was designed in bold, solid checks of black and white, running together just now with dark brown liquid. Ushering would be in open collar today.

"My race tie, too, durn it all!" exclaimed Jimmy. "Only wear it once a year—can't next week, 'course—I'll be at the track!"

That much I had already figured. It was painfully clear to everyone that Jimmy hadn't missed a race in seventeen years and that the single blemish on his otherwise untarnished record was due to a mishap on a motorcycle that had landed him a two-month hospital stay. Back from there, he'd been at every race since kindergarten. Several others in the church could best his mark by several laps around the calendar year, including Skip Henderson, Clyde Parsens, and Jimmy's own uncle Sarge, who hadn't missed since he returned from Korea. But they were courteous enough to display their attendance trophies down on a lower shelf.

From May first onward, Jimmy's fervor for racing accelerated like speeds at the track, as engines and spirits were tweaked for the holiest of unholy days of the year. Jimbo wasn't alone, of course. Race fever, as it was popularly called, spread each spring like a social disease, until every known form of resistance was taxed to the very verge of capitulation.

The fever was undoubtedly the culprit in Jimmy's Sunday-morning brush with death by church commute. One of countless out-of-towners on race pilgrimage had been out performing his sabbath rites. In his jacked-up Chevy Malibu, with dual quads and racing spoiler, he had pulled out brazenly into Jimmy's path and then proceeded to cruise like a pace car under a yellow flag. Before you could say, "Lord, help me!" Jimmy had strapped on his helmet and pushed it to the floor, passing him at 70 mph and cutting in again as close as a shave. The Malibu, by now in the full frenzy of worship, cranked up the rpm's and prepared to leave Jimmy's Ford in a pillar of cloud. Jimmy was moving to block him when Jennifer grabbed the wheel in the rage of holy terror. As the Malibu came around, its driver jerked the wheel hard right, intending this time to run them clean off the road. At the last possible moment, Jimmy had come to his senses, giving the brakes so definitive a slam that the dashboard coffee-cup holder broke free from its glue stick. Already lukewarm, the coffee had not only doused Jimmy's Sunday best but lowered his track temperature considerably.

"I hate Chevy!" Jimmy said, resting his case.

The whole narrative left me more than a little squeamish, but over eleven months of ministry I had trained myself not to react to accounts like these. It was better to remain coolly aloof in a pastoral sort of way. Tall Kentucky tales keep out a watchful eye for their next victim. Strong reactions to such stories, even the truthful ones, only led to the increased likelihood of having to endure more of the same in the future. Life situations in which true change was possible were almost always of the more mundane, less colorful variety.

"Been to the track yet this year?" I asked, wondering if I'd even listen to his answer, noting that I didn't seem to care one way or the other.

"Time trials . . . couple days a' qualifications . . . I like Mears to win again. Guy's amazin'! . . . Oughta come, Preacher! Not fair it's goin' on 'n' yer stuck here! . . . Maybe yeh oughta cancel church. Them churches down in Speedway do! No way them people's gettin' anywhere Sunday mornin'! Heck, they're prob'ly rentin' out their lawns fer parkin'.''

"They're probably going to the race!" I added.

"No kiddin' there, Bud. Hey, think about it. Might still git yeh a ticket—never know," he added doubtfully.

Over the course of the month, the seed of the possibility of canceling worship had been sown countless times by numerous people. In this case, it was the seed that fell along the path and was trampled underfoot. I had no intention of scratching church to placate guilty consciences—just in case there might have been any. Religion in America was quickly becoming a battle of the venues. In the great societal search for some new and elusive spiritual high, no rock was being left unturned. In theaters and auditoriums, stadiums and arenas, storefronts and sweat lodges, out in the woods and down by the sea, the masses were gathering in the name of whomever they chose for a fix of whatever they sought.

Once a year in Indianapolis, on Memorial weekend appropriately, all combatants in this war of the venues called a truce. All deferred, willingly or not, to the greatest spectacle in racing, the Speedway, the 500, the Majestic Oval, the Track. It could gobble up a score of major league baseball parks, encompass a dozen football stadiums, and accommodate on its grounds six Vatican Cities at once. For many years, the 500 had been run on Memorial Day—May 30th—but that was product of a bygone era, when even the hardest core race fans would coast past a church and bow their heads to the Lord Jesus at the perfunctory pre-race prayer. This had all come to a crashing halt in the early '70s, when the race was moved permanently to Sunday. There were few voices to challenge an institution as venerable as most congregations, and those who had tried were easily drowned out in the drone of engines at the starting line. Still, the vast majority of churches continued on with their normal patterns of worship, though Memorial weekend services rivaled "Low Sunday," the second of Easter, as most lightly attended of the year. While I was pastor at any rate, Ashgrove Baptist was not about to desert the cause. Whatever else I might be in the way of wishy-washy, I was no liturgical turncoat.

Jimmy telephoned that Thursday evening with the miraculous news of a spare ticket. Further inquiry uncovered that the ticket belonged to Jennifer, who was all fevered out and had announced that *she* at least would be going to church. Jennifer was a lifelong Baptist. She had met Jimmy, a lifelong non-Baptist, in their early thirties. In her race against biological time, Jennifer had entered into the marital contract under the illusion of many that people will change to accommodate the wishes of others.

Five barren years and much teeth gnashing later, she had mended little in Jimmy but much in her thinking on the subject. It was true that he had become a duly baptized church member. He even ushered two Sundays a month. But the hard habits were too deeply ingrained for her sandpaper tactics to wear away. So Jennifer had begun to address her own behavior, instead. All else in her life she professed to have surrendered to the Great Carpenter himself. I thankfully declined Jimmy's kind offer but did take the opportunity to ask Jennifer to usher in Jimmy's absence. She accepted, gladly.

The only momentous decision still before me was a race-day route to the church. My wife, Donna, and I resided fifteen miles distant on the city's near northeast side. On race morning, tens of thousands of automobiles descended upon the west side of Indianapolis, like ants on a dish of dog food. Finding a course from the east across Speedway was on a level of difficulty roughly equivalent to escaping into West Berlin before the wall came tumbling down. To help clarify things for me, I was offered more maps and verbal route instructions than AAA prepares nationwide in a week.

"Here, Preacher: Head north up to Fifty-sixth and then west *across* the Interstate. Continue on, all the way out of town to County Road 200 east, then double back on Rockville Road to the county line."

"Go south and get on 70 west, heading out of town. Take it to the State Road 267 exit at Plainville, then turn east, back into the county on U.S. 40."

"Some say yeh can do okay on Michigan Street, and smaller streets around, and snake yeh a path right through town—but leave early, by 6:00 A.M.!"

"I'd stay overnight at church if I was you—better yet, come spend the night with us!—Even get yeh an early breakfast before we head down to the track!"

In the end, I chose Fifty-sixth Street, leaving at exactly 7:30. My wife, Donna, was staffing on day shift at the hospital and had left the house just as the gates at Speedway were opening. I was going solo. Traffic was surprisingly light, and by the time I got to the interstate, it was only 7:45. Crossing the overpass and looking south toward the track, I observed only the normal stream of traffic—no thousand-car pile-ups, no bumpers colliding, no horns sounding the purgatorial angst of rush-hour traffic jams. All seemed eerily serene and quiet.

"Where are all the cars? What's happened?" I heard myself query. I flipped on the radio to "the voice of the 500," but it was airing commercials as always. Then, in an inexplicable derailment of rationality—the closest I've ever come to race fever—I abandoned Fifty-sixth Street, hopped onto the interstate, and headed south into oblivion.

"I'll just take it to Thirty-eighth Street," I reassured myself, "see what's going on, then head west again."

At precisely 7:48 A.M., I ran into the biggest wall of automotive metal ever amassed. An hour later, the sign read, "Thirty-eighth

Street—2 miles." After one hour and forty-five minutes, my
odometer had advanced three-tenths of a mile. The teacher was
about to be a no-show at his own adult Sunday school class. "No
one'll be there anyway!" I consoled myself through the mount-
ing anxiety. At 10:29 A.M., with a minute to spare before worship,
I was cleared for take-off onto a slow ramp up to west Thirty-
eighth Street. Twenty-two minutes later, I pulled into the gravel
drive and scrambled to the door of Ashgrove Church. To my
great shock, there was Jimmy, a stack of bulletins in his hands,
and a checkerboard necktie with so faint a streak of brown it
required a certain piece of modern folklore even to notice it.
Jennifer was opposite him at the sanctuary doors, cradling her
own stack of bulletins and smiling ear to ear.

"His truck wouldn't start," she explained. "Everyone he
knows who was goin' was already gone. Durn shame, in't it? . . .
told him we was gonna be walkin' over here more often!"

"I hate Ford!" was all Jimmy could manage.

I climbed into the pulpit at 11:25 and preached a reasonably
strong if somewhat distracted message from Philippians on the
faithful race of the upward call of God, which overcomes set-
backs, tragedy, and even death itself. From the back pew, Jimmy's
boom box, though at a reverently low setting, managed to keep
the holy pilgrims informed of that other race's progress. In his
Chevy Indy, Emerson Fittipaldi had just taken the lead on lap
ninety-three. Rick Mears, in a Chevy of his own, had experienced
engine trouble all through the first half of racing. In the pole
position, he had been widely anticipated to earn back to back
victories. Instead, Fittipaldi, his archrival of the previous year,
whom he had beaten under an anticlimactic yellow flag, was
snatching victory away. The Unsers and Andrettis were also in
the hunt as usual, but the crowds held out for their beloved
Mears to come back.

There were over 400,000 in attendance at the greatest spectacle in racing. When I had shown up, our numbers had climbed
to forty-four. Meanwhile, eighty-eight ears strained in the contest
for attention, a regional skirmish in a wider war of allegiances.
And then, as Mears was coming out of the backstretch on lap one
hundred and seventeen, his linkage went out, right out there,
halfway along the path to glory. His Formula One miracle machine rolled to a halt, to the sound of a great, collective sigh that
stretched out even as far as country pews twelve miles way.

The sermon gave out at about the same time. We sang a hymn. I gave the benediction and stood at the sanctuary door to greet the hard-core faithful. Last in line was Jimmy. He'd gone to the kitchen refrigerator and brought back a tall glass of milk. He pushed it up to my face.

"Here, I think yeh earned this today! . . ." I looked at him quizzically. "Just drink it!" he said, "It's a joke. . . . But yer a preacher. You'll probably never figure it out. . . ."

For the last quarter of the race, a dozen of us sat in the vestibule, hovering over Jimmy's boom box. Jimmy supplemented the radio commentary like a frenzied prophet who can envisage clearly what his proselytes are only now hearing for the first time. The race ended once again under yellow, a sweet irony for the triumphant Fittipaldi. He drove into the winner's circle and drank down a whole ceremonial cow of the white liquid. And then, the greatest spectacle in the cosmos was over.

A remarkable run in racing had come to an end. It would take Jimmy to the year 2004—or well into his fifties—to recover and possibly overtake that brilliant seventeen-year attendance mark. But I had every faith he would succeed, as I watched him and Jennifer start out together on their four blessed feet, down the long, country road toward home.

25

Quilting Bee

Patchwork Sabbath

For everything there is a season,
and a time for every matter under heaven:
a time to be born, and a time to die;
a time to plant, and a time to pluck up what is planted;
. . . a time to weep, and a time to laugh;
. . . a time to seek, and a time to lose;
a time to keep, and a time to throw away;
a time to tear, and a time to sew. . . .
Ecclesiastes 3:1–7

At Ashgrove Church, the first day of the week was Tuesday. Once I understood this, I was greatly relieved. Like many, I had spent most of my life confused as to whether Sunday, the day of rest, began or ended the week. As on numerous scores, the good people of Ashgrove were kind enough to alleviate my anxiety on the subject once and for all. Monday—"blue Monday"—was really nothing to fear. It was only a filler, a simple bridge from the Sabbath to a new week's real genesis—Tuesday. Wishing to be one among the people, I quickly adopted their unique pattern as my own, taking Monday as my personal day of rest. Then, like Tuesday's namesake, Tyr, the Norse god of war, I purposed to take the bold new week by storm. I began to set my alarm for a very early hour on Tuesdays, in order to arrive at the church by 8:00 A.M. But it was never soon enough—not by a long shot.

On the first day, God had said, "Let there be quilters!" And so there were quilters, about eight in number, who arrived at the

little grove on Tuesdays with the first light of dawn. Immediately
they took command of the affairs of state, or of stitching at any
rate. They were like knights at court, but their roundtable was a
rectangular quilting frame, and from it they wielded their needles, threads, and thimbles with authority. It was understood and
accepted that men would occupy the visible seats of power in the
church. The deacon and trustee boards had always been male-
led, male-dominated entities. But none was deluded as to the
source, after the Lord himself, of ultimate influence. The
quilters were queen bees; church officers were their soldiers and
drones. As in many marriages, Ashgrove Church took its shape
and purpose from a matriarchal center. The very spirit and soul
of a community of faith emanated from a large wooden frame
in the fellowship hall on Tuesday mornings.

When I entered the building on a typical Tuesday, the
quilters had already stitched minutes together into hours. I
made it a point to greet them immediately, hoping to appear
rushed with matters of urgency and importance, but this was to
no avail. They rarely even looked up to acknowledge my arrival.

"*Mornin'*, Preacher," was the extent of their greeting. This
was delivered in such a fashion that the interrogative, "*Is* it still
mornin'?" never failed to linger in the air. Then I would pause
for a brief, unbelieving interval, straining to recall what I had
concluded when last I had witnessed that same scene. As the
quilters leaned forward, their heads bowed low, their hands
outstretched, one over and one under a great sheet, they brought
to mind either the Mennonites at prayer or a witches' coven. I
believe, in fact, it must have been a good bit of both. . . . .

Each of the quilters had learned the craft from her mother.
It had been passed down with the same ardor all mothers feel
toward their daughters on their wedding days or at the birth of a
first grandchild. Their depth of sentiment on the subject appeared bottomless. Indeed, the quilters harbored a deep anxiety
over the future. Quilters gauged the state of the world and all
millennial prospects by the number of their own daughters and
kin who were plying the craft. When there were no longer any
quilters, they believed, when there was no one left anywhere to
weave garments of warmth and comfort and hope in a cold-
hearted and cruel world, then the end would come. The Son of
Man would descend in the clouds. The last trumpet would
sound, summoning from their graves all weavers, crocheters,

knitters, darners, and quilters to the great loom in the sky. There, no babes would cry for lack of swaddle, neither would the elderly shiver through any night. For all would rest warm and secure, safely tucked under a blanket of grace—God's genial fleece of everlasting favor.

Meanwhile, the quilters carried on the work of the kingdom coming. Most of them used thimbles on thumbs or index fingers. A few chose to work unprotected, like motorcyclists without helmets or carpenters without safety glasses. There were no laws on the books to govern such acts of daring. Thimble or no, all of the quilters had developed over time an eerie affinity for the lot of a pincushion. Yet the blood they spilled was not the blood of martyrdom, but of destiny, they believed. While some of its drops landed on the tile floor to be commingled with the past, others stained the new fabric of the age just coming. Through opened veins, they held time itself in their hands.

The quilters could go a coon's age without missing a Tuesday around the wooden frame. Only once during my stay at Ashgrove Church, a winter day when the roads were especially icy, did the quilters fail to meet. Somehow I had managed to make it in to the church that particular morning, and I lived to regret it. It was an especially chilly day. The heat pump carried on its high-pitched groaning like a lonely whale in captivity. No aroma wafted from the kitchen to augur well the comfort of a noon hour repast. Instead, I ate bologna. Worst of all, I heard no matronly voices in the background, uttering bad theology with uncommon conviction. It was an abysmally boring day from beginning to end.

The quilters of Ashgrove disagreed often amongst themselves, but they never quarreled. You don't jerk in a fit of rage while pointing a sharp needle in your direction from close range. I have thought that quilting diplomacy would be a prudent strategy in the arena of global politics. Imagine heads of state holding summits around a giant quilting frame. The belligerents in a conflict could sew from opposite ends and meet in the middle. "Summitry by Symmetry," they could call it "Design a quilt while resolving the nastiest squabbles on the world stage. Do it with needle point rather than at swords' points. Visualize the conflict, employing image therapy. Take home a souvenir of the triumph of reason and creativity over antagonism and hostility."

Well, one wonders. . . . .

Following a full morning's stitching, the quilters feasted. Recipes as old as the hills were served and swapped. New ones were concocted and judged to be successes or failures. Greens, cornbread, and potatoes of all kinds were favorites. Anything with lard was an instant triumph. I was fortunate to have early developed a wide palate. Indeed, I was delighted when the ladies took me on as a project, determined to fatten me up like the Christmas goose. At noon I was summoned to the table and instructed to return thanks. Once I adjusted to the company, this was the easiest assignment of the week.

One Tuesday during a quilting bee, the most significant event of my pastorate occurred. The ladies had just completed a section of quilt and were engaged in the arduous task of turning the material to the next section on the frame. The frame had to be loosened and the quilt carefully repositioned. Then, with their farm-bred grips, the quilters would stretch the material as tautly as possible across the frame and clamp it tightly into place. They had the method down to a fine science, of course, but on that particular day they were uncharacteristically shy on elbow grease.

"Tarnation!" shot up Alberta Rump. "Told you ladies a hundred times there ain't no use a' doin' this without some dinner down us first!"

"Now, Bert," Gladys said, "you know them potatoes and that beef needs some more time to simmer into stew—so *you* just simmer down, and we'll make out just fine!"

Only Gladys Hatch got away with such fiery talk fed to combustible Bert. They hailed from the same hills in southeastern Kentucky and were even rumored to be distant cousins, though neither spoke of it. But Gladys understood her. Once she found that Bert indeed had a pulse, she had put her finger there and never taken it off. Even so, to hear Gladys's retort made me a little jittery. Just at that moment I had been walking past them to the kitchen for a mid-morning cup of coffee.

"Maybe the preacher would like to help!" Madge Spires had blurted out abruptly. Madge was the most elderly of the quilters. From the time of my arrival, she had been more openly suspicious of me than most. She had even quizzed me about my drinking habits.

"Me?" I had asked in feigned astonishment. "You're asking your pastor if *he drinks?*"

Madge had known this was not an answer. She had simply stared at me and put me on notice that she did not believe in that sort of thing.

Now, for perhaps the first time in Ashgrove quilting history, all the ladies were staring at the pastor at once.

"Me?" I uttered in astonishment, but this time sounding like the last boy chosen for the pickup softball game. "You want *my help?*"

"Think you wouldn't mind?" asked Gladys politely.

"I'll be glad to try!"

The significance of this moment was lost on no one. I was being invited into the inner sanctum of restricted faith. It was like a Muslim woman gaining access to a mosque. Such opportunities do not come around every day, certainly not in ordained ministry. I was determined to make the most of it.

The quilters positioned me in the center of the frame. I was flanked by Millie Grimshaw and her niece by marriage, Jenny Grimshaw, who was almost as new to quilting as I. Directly across from me was Bert, who had brought north from Kentucky the strongest grip in the Cumberland Mountains—black bears not excepted. Our task was to twist the fabric over the frame in a roll until it was taut enough to clamp into place. With the experienced guidance of Madge and Gladys, the feat was accomplished in no time. Madge nodded in approval. Bert winked. Briefly I imagined the Ashgrove quilters and I were as tight as the frame. Though the feeling was fleeting, and though I was never again called up to active quilting duty, I regarded this event as the turning point of my pastorate.

Every pastoral appointment has its formal rites of passage, occasions by which pastor and people mark the progress or regress of their joint sojourn. There is the day of installation and anniversary years—first, fifth, tenth, and so on. There are old-home days and red-letter days, jubilees, and homecomings. There are also seasons of conflict in every marriage of pastor and people, often making or breaking the relationship, but shaping it willy-nilly. The day the quilters requested my participation in a ritual quilt-turning was the day I came to belong to Ashgrove Baptist Church. In some ways, that Tuesday—the first day of the week, mind you—was the first day of my pastorate.

Toward the end of my tenure at Ashgrove Church, the quilters fell uncharacteristically silent. They had begun a new and bold quilt in the wedding ring pattern. Often, their quilts were intended as gifts for children and friends, or for occasions such as weddings or births. However, I was aware of no weddings pending, either in the church or among the church's extended families. The work progressed under a conspiracy of silence, with my attentions by and large focused elsewhere.

When the quilt neared completion, I began to pay it greater heed. It consisted of interlocking circles, each fashioned from strips of recycled fabric cut into wedges. Fabric patterns included polka dots, pieces of fruit, florals, and gingham. One pattern featuring roosters took me back indeterminately to my childhood. There were fifteen or twenty patterns in all, each appearing and reappearing at random throughout the quilt. To the larger scheme of intersecting circles, they added another tier of unity amid diversity. Here was the great circle of life combined with the eternal bond of love and highlighted by recurring splashes of color and form. Here was truth, beauty, and goodness, virtue itself, charged with a task of highest utility: to bring warmth to life. All had been painstakingly pieced and sewed together before the quilters positioned it over batting and had at it. Then, as quickly as it had ascended to the frame, the finished quilt disappeared and another took its place.

A month of Tuesdays and Sundays passed. On the first day of the Ashgrove week, a real August scorcher, I was preparing to sit down to dinner with the quilters when my wife arrived. She had left work early on the invitation to join us. As my head bobbed up after prayer, Gladys was coming from the kitchen with a cake and five lighted candles. Bert was right behind her, bearing a ridiculous grin and a gift that she delivered into Donna's hands. It was our fifth anniversary of marriage. Before Donna ever reached the large box and lifted the lid, I knew what it contained.

A dozen years have elapsed since the wedding-ring quilt came home to stay. It is draped over a rack in our guest room, a token of hospitality extended to all visitors and a sure hedge against the deep-winter chill. Over that time, we have moved once and added four children to the family roster. With each new addition, a small quilt has arrived from the Tuesday faithful, God's co-agents in the work of creation. Rachael and Rebecca, Seth and Sarah have each felt their warm, plush embrace. These emblems of endearment are the strongest ties that bind us yet to the sleepy grove of maple and ash.

And quilting, too, will endure. The life expectancy of cotton fabric is perhaps two hundred years under the most favorable conditions. For only a few fleeting years longer will any of Ashgrove's stalwart practitioners of the craft escape the grave. But quilting itself will live on, down at least the length of a civilization with an already tenuous grip on longevity. As long as there are wars and rumors of war, which strip, cripple, and maim, as long as there is drafty air and winter's biting frost, then there will be quilters to wrap and shelter bodies, to bind and mend hearts. It is a first-order reality, as certain as that God brought light from darkness and day from the cold black night.

> I know that whatever God does endures forever; nothing can be added to it, nor anything taken from it; God has done this, so that all should stand in awe before him. That which is, already has been; that which is to be, already is; and God seeks out what has gone by.
>
> Ecclesiastes 3:14–15